CW00868055

The Poppy Trilogy

Angela Taylor

Published by Angela Taylor
Publishing partner: Paragon Publishing, Rothersthorpe
First published 2019
© Angela Taylor 2019

Cover photographs: Pixabay

ISBN 978-1-78222-705-2

Book design, layout and production management by Into Print
www.intoprint.net
+44 (0)1604 832149

Contents

Guardian of the Key

1

Poppy had her first sight of their new home as the car came to a halt beside the removal van. The men were already busy unloading their possessions. Poppy looked in amazement at what her father had described as a farmhouse. The roof dipped at one end, and the chimneys were the tallest Poppy had ever seen.

'Well girls, what do you think of our house?' Their mother asked anxiously.

'Oh Mum, it's lovely,' said Poppy.

'What about you Lily, do you think you will like it here?'

'No Mum, I won't, you know I didn't want to leave London and my friends.' With a scowl on her face she picked up her bag and marched into the house. Her parents sighed; they were used to Lily's teenage outbursts. Poppy said she was off to explore the house and choose her bedroom. At least their youngest daughter seemed delighted with the move.

They had been shocked when their parents announced that they were moving to an isolated farmhouse in the Suffolk countryside. It didn't soften the blow when their father said the beach was only a mile away and they could have friends to stay in the holidays.

Poppy was happily putting away her clothes when she heard muffled sounds coming from Lily's room. She opened her sister's door to find her sitting on the floor crying.

'Don't cry Lily we'll soon make friends at the new school and I'm sure there are clubs we can join.'

Lily dried her eyes and hugged her sister.

'I'm being selfish, let's get on with the unpacking, mum said we can have a day on the beach tomorrow if we work hard today.'

The following morning their mother gave them a hand drawn map. It showed a track through the pine woods which would bring them out on the beach. It was a hot day so they wore swimming costumes under their shorts and tee shirts and set off on their bikes. It was easy to find the track through the woods and in spite of the bumpy ride they were soon on the beach. They stripped off their outer clothes and ran across the hot sand boldly jumping into the water, unaware that the North Sea is freezing cold even on the hottest summers day.

Lily braved the cold and continued swimming but Poppy came out straight away and was searching for shells when she was startled to find an elderly woman suddenly at her side. She was tall and thin and wore a bright green cloak around her shoulders. Her silver hair was short and spiked and glistened in the sun.

'Good morning,' she said with a smile that didn't quite reach her eyes. 'I believe you have just moved into the manor house. I'm Mrs. Beddows, your nearest neighbour. What is your name child?'

Poppy was mesmerized by the piercing eyes and

replied softly that her name was Poppy. The old woman's face took on a cat like appearance as her eyes reduced to mere slits. Her head on one side she looked quizzically at Poppy and muttered something quietly to herself and then turned abruptly and walked away towards the woods.

What a strange woman thought Poppy.

Hearing Lily call, she turned and ran down the beach to meet her.

'Who were you talking to?' Lily asked.

'Her name is Mrs. Beddows, and I'm sure she is a witch, she has green and yellow eyes and when I told her my name she muttered something which sounded like "a flower guards the key".

Lily laughed,

'You must be light-headed, I think you need some lunch, I know I do, I'm starving after that swim. I'll race you back.'

Cycling along the track through the woods, Poppy looked from side to side, sure they were being watched and fully expecting to see Mrs. Beddows appear from behind one of the trees at any moment. At one point she nearly fell off her bike in fright when a bird flew out of a nearby bush. Peddling for all she was worth, she caught up with Lily as she reached the road.

They wheeled their bikes up the gravel drive and around the back of the house to the shed where their father was neatly storing away his gardening tools. Poppy told him of her meeting with Mrs. Beddows with Lily butting in to say they had a witch for a neighbour. He said that he hadn't heard of anyone by that name in the neighbourhood. Closing the shed door, he asked them to go and give their mother a hand so that she could get lunch ready.

They found their mother in the hall sorting out packing cases. Leaving her daughters to move the boxes into the lounge she went to prepare lunch. Lily picked up a large box and took it into the lounge. Poppy carried the lighter board games but tripped on the uneven floorboards and dropped the lot. The dice from the Ludo set rolled away down the slopping floor and disappeared under the skirting board.

When Lily returned all she saw was Poppy's bottom up in the air and her headclose to the floor as she tried to squeeze her fingers between the floorboards and skirting to reach the dice. Lily un-bent a wire coat hanger which soon did the trick, the dice and what appeared to be a very old key came from under the skirting covered in dust.

'I wonder what door this belongs to?' Poppy asked.

'It's too small for a door, I should think it belongs to a box or piece of furniture and I'm sure that it's made of silver,' replied Lily.

'It's rather pretty, I think I'll slip my silver chain through it and wear it around my neck,' said Poppy.

At lunch their parents told them they had decided to hold a barbeque the following week to meet their new neighbours and that they could invite their friends from London. The evening was spent writing out their invitations but when their mother caught Poppy yawning she suggested an early night. Poppy was just dropping off to sleep when she heard her name being called through the open window. She looked out into the moonlit garden, was that a movement in the shrubbery, someone standing in the shadows? She sighed in relief when a cat walked out onto the lawn, stretched out its back legs and walked away around the side of the house. She got back into bed and was sound asleep in no time at all.

2

The following week passed quickly, the weather had been good; they had swum and explored the surrounding countryside. When their friends arrived on the Saturday they soon pitched in to help set out tables and chairs and hang lanterns on the trellis around the patio. Their father got the barbeque going; sausages, beef burgers and chicken drum sticks were piled up waiting for the charcoal to get hot. A large pan of sliced onions were frying gently; filling the air with a mouth-watering aroma. The youngsters enjoyed themselves dancing to loud music whilst Lily and Poppy's parents made friends with the elderly vicar and his wife and Miss Meredith. The latter lived in a cottage down the lane from the farmhouse and the girls were told that Miss Meredith would be teaching them at their new school.

Poppy had found a quiet corner as she didn't want anyone to notice she was on her third hotdog when Mrs. Beddows appeared at her elbow. Poppy jumped and bit rather quickly through the hotdog causing half to fall to the ground leaving buttery onions to slide down her chin. Poppy was annoyed she had been enjoying those onions. Mrs. Beddows took her by the arm.

'I know you are the new guardian of the key, I want you to show me that you have it safe.' Poppy looked at her in amazement thinking the old girl must be bats.

She remembered the key she had found and wondered if that could be the one Mrs. Beddows wanted.

'I don't know what you are talking about,' said Poppy.

The old lady put an icy cold hand on Poppy's warm arm.

'I know you have the key. I dreamt many years ago that a flower would guard the key, but it's mine and I want it back,' she said her voice sounding menacing to Poppy's ear. Poppy pushed her arm away and ran screaming across the lawn to her parents.

'What on earth's the matter Poppy?' asked her father.

Her mother gathered her into her arms as Poppy sobbed.

'It's Mrs. Beddows, she wants the silver key that I found.'

'Mrs. Beddows, who is she?'

'We told Dad all about her, she's a witch and a neighbour and you invited her to the barbeque,' Poppy cried.

'I've never heard of a Mrs. Beddows, nor did I invite her tonight.'

'That's strange, a woman of that name lived in Miss Meredith's cottage over a hundred years ago and the locals said that she was a witch, but of course we don't believe in witches nowadays do we?' the vicar commented.

'I found a trunk of very old books in my attic when I moved in and several have the name of Naomi Beddows written on the flyleaf. Come and look through them tomorrow, it might throw a light on the mystery,' said Miss Meredith to Poppy and Lily.

'Your friend's parents have just arrived to collect

them and I think it's time we got you girls tucked safely into bed,' said their father.

Next morning Poppy came downstairs with the key on a chain around her neck. The girls had a hurried breakfast and set off down the lane.

Miss Meredith was working in her garden. On seeing the girls she downed her tools and ushered them inside and up the stairs to the attic. They dragged the trunk over to the window and brushed the dust from the lid. Their fingers struggled with the thick leather straps which were cracked and hard with age. Finally managing to undo them they lifted the lid and took the books out, examining them carefully as the pages were very thin. Miss Meredith reached into the trunk for the last item which was wrapped in sacking. She opened it to reveal a large book, the covers of which were made of thick silver with a keyhole set into a strong clasp.

Poppy took the chain from around her neck.

'Look, the front cover has the same design as the key,' she said fitting the key into the keyhole. The clasp fell open and Miss Meredith turned the thick parchment pages.

'Goodness, I think it's a book of spells,' she gasped in surprise.

They peered over her shoulder to see drawings and strange lists of words written in spidery hand writing.

'There, what did I say, Mrs. Beddows must be a witch and somehow or other she lost the key to her spell book, gabbled an excited Poppy.

'Yes and when she met you on the beach and heard your name she knew you would have the key so she gate crashed our barbeque to try and get it back,' Lily stated.

'I think we should take this to the vicar for safe keeping,' said Miss Meredith rewrapping the book. The three of them set out immediately and were lucky enough to find the vicar in the church. The vicar frowned as he looked at the contents of the book, relocked it quickly and placed it on the top shelf of a strong cupboard that housed the parish records. He removed the heavy key from the oak door and put it in his pocket.

'That should do the trick. If Mrs. Beddows is a witch she won't come onto consecrated ground.'

'I believe you are meant to be the keeper of the silver key, please keep it safe,' the vicar said handing the dainty key and chain back to Poppy who quickly replaced it around her neck. She looked up at the vicar and asked,

'Are there really witches and ghosts?'

The vicar smiled at the girls and replied,

'Only the good Lord knows.'

3

It was early September and Lily was wheeling her bicycle out of the shed and calling for Poppy to hurry up.

Poppy dashed out of the kitchen with a piece of toast between her teeth as she tried to hoist her school bag over her back.

'It won't do to be late on our first day,' Lily said as she watched Poppy struggling to heave her bicycle over the shed's threshold and catching the chain on the door leaving behind an oily gouge.

'Dad's not going to be very pleased when he sees *that*.'

'Well, you could have helped me instead of nagging,' Poppy said crossly.

At the end of the gravel drive sat a black cat, it watched as they mounted their bicycles and followed them out of the gate.

'That cat's been hanging around our house since the day we moved in. I hope it isn't scratching in those new flowerbeds Dad made,' said Lily.

Poppy looked warily at the cat. It was ridiculous but she had the feeling that it had been keeping an eye on her since that first night that it had appeared in the garden. She wasn't going to admit that to Lily though.

There was a chill wind in the air and the sky was overcast as they peddled furiously towards Leiston which was a mile and a half away.

'It's hard to believe that we were sunning ourselves on the beach two days ago,' sighed Lily as she free wheeled with her legs held out so that she could inspect her tan.

'Mum said it's not healthy to get sunburnt,' replied Poppy looking at her own white legs. Lily gave her a scornful look.

This was the first time that they had cycled to Leiston, usually they went by car with their mother on the weekly shopping trip. Their heads were bent against the wind as they approached the red brick school where a huge bell swung from a high turret. When Poppy first saw the school in the summer she had thought that it looked like a great ship sailing amidst a sea of waving corn.

Lily was slightly ahead of her sister when without warning a boy cycled out of a side lane without looking and cannoned into Lily knocking her onto the ground.

'YOU CLUMSY OAF! don't you know you are supposed to give way at junctions? I would have thought you were old enough to know your Highway Code by now,' she roared.

The boy was of a stocky build with an untidy mop of black hair and when he spoke it was with a broad Suffolk accent.

'OK, Miss Hoity toity, with the posh accent, keep your hair on, no harm done,' he said as he turned in at the school gates without bothering to help her.

'What a rude boy,' said Poppy as she laid her bicycle down and offered her sister a hand to help her up. Lily brushed the sandy dirt from her clothes and dabbed a handkerchief to her grazed knee but it was obvious she was trying hard to keep the tears at bay.

'I'm ok, we had better get a move on.'

They stowed their bicycles into the rack and joined the queue filing in at the open double doors. They soon found the secretary's office and in answer to Lily's knock, a friendly voice asked them to come in.

Mrs. Allen, the secretary said that she would introduce Poppy to her class and teacher first. Lily watched in envy as her sister entered the class eagerly. All Lily felt as she climbed the stairs beside Mrs. Allen was apprehension.

Miss Meredith opened the door to their knock, smiled a welcome at Lily and indicated a seat halfway up the room. Sitting in the seat directly behind was the rude boy from outside the gates. He pulled a face at her when Miss Meredith's back was turned and Lily knew that things could only get worse.

She was relieved when lunch time came as she had quietly endured a morning of being poked in the back with a ruler, had her long hair tugged viciously and rubber bands flicked at her. She knew it wouldn't do to complain to Miss Meredith, nobody liked a snitch. To make matters worse the senior pupils used a separate playground from the younger ones who also had first sitting for lunch so Lily resigned herself to eating on her own.

She put her books in her bag and started to leave the classroom when the boy who sat on her right said,

'I'm Toby Richards, would you like to eat your lunch with me and Melanie?' He pointed to a pretty blonde girl who sat at the back of the class.

16

'Jed Briggs won't be able to annoy you with us around.'

'Oh thanks, that would be great.'

Toby introduced Lily to Melanie as they made their way to the playground where they were lucky enough to find an empty bench to sit on.

Lily described the incident when Jed had knocked her off her bike.

'He didn't have the good manners to stop and help me up either.'

'Just stand up to him whenever he confronts you, he'll soon stop when he realises he can't bully you,' said Melanie.

'Have you only just moved into the area?' asked Toby.

Lily told them of their move from London and how her young sister had already had an encounter with a strange women whom they thought was a witch. Toby and Melanie begged her to tell them all about this so called witch and stared in disbelief as Lily's story unfolded.

'With your first-hand experience of witches, you should try auditioning for a part in our end of term play,' said Toby.

'The part of a witch you mean? Is that how you see me and what parts are you two after?'

'I want to play Mac and Melanie wants the part of Beastly Beth.'

'What's this played called then?'

'Mac the knife,' said Toby and Melanie laughing.

'I know, it's really Shakespere's *Macbeth* isn't it?

'Yes, you're right and I don't think you look at all like a witch but I'm sure you could act the part easily. Will

17

you come with us for the auditions tonight then?' asked Toby.

The bell rang for second sitting lunch and the three got up to join the queue into the dining hall.

'Come on Lily, give us an answer,' said Melanie.

Lily smiled at them both and said, 'OK, I'll give it a try.'

The end of day bell sounded, Lily quickly stuffed her books and pens into her bag; told Toby and Melanie that she must find Poppy first and that she would meet up with them in the hall.

Poppy already had her bike out of the rack and was scanning the busy playground for her sister when Lily rushed up out of ' ....ppy replaced her bike in the rack after hea. .... auditions and followed Lily, happy to sit and .... 'ry her hand at acting.

The din in the hall w .... ous as would be actors quoted lines from Macbeth to impress each other and argued over who wanted what part. Lily made her way through the crowd and introduced Poppy to her new friends. Toby made a friend for life when he smiled at her and told her she could watch them and be their first critic.

Miss Wells, the drama teacher, entered the hall and clapped her hands for silence. Melanie nudged Lily as she noticed Jed Briggs edging to the front of the stage.

'He thinks he is going to get the part of Mac, but he isn't as good as Toby,' whispered Melanie to Lily.

Poppy sat on a bench against the wall and enjoyed watching and listening as the pupils read their lines from the script for the part they wished to play.

Miss Wells gave auditions for the smaller parts first,

which included Lily who gave a good performance as one of the three old witches. As Lily left the stage Jed Briggs was heard to snigger to his pals that Lily didn't need to act for the part of a witch. Poor Lily's face flushed beetroot red as she hurried back to her friends with her head down.

'Take no notice, you were great,' said Toby.

Melanie took her place in a line of four girls for the part of Beastly Beth and then it was Toby's turn to try for the part of Mac. He was obviously the favourite as the girls in his form clapped enthusiastically when he finished and Melanie looked as proud as punch.

Jed Briggs performance was not so polished and only his friends cheered for him.

Auditions over, Miss Wells told everyone to help themselves to a glass of the lemonade provided whilst she decided who got what part.

There were shouts of joy and one or two tears as the various name___ ___ally read out. Lily was pleased when she he___ ___e called out for the part of one of the witch___ ___nie was delighted to be chosen for Beastly beth.

Of course Toby got the part of Mac and if looks could kill then the look on Jed Briggs's face would have laid Toby out on the floor. Passing Toby to leave the hall with his friends he spluttered out,

'I'll get my own back on you Toby Richards, if it's the last thing I do.'

Toby told them as they got their bikes from the shed, that he wasn't worried by Jed's threats. They called goodbye to each other at the school gates to cycle their separate ways home. Poppy told Lily she thought she had glimpsed Jed Briggs talking to someone in the high bracken outside the gates; someone who wore bright green.

Lily didn't reply, thinking to herself that there had been much too much talk of witches that day.

4

'Lily, if you want to buy the material for your witches costume, you had better get a move on,' her mother called.

Lily picked up her bag, dashed down the stairs and out of the house, slamming the door behind her. She ran through the pile of leaves which her father had just raked up, jumped into the car breathing heavily and plonked herself down beside her sister.

'Lily,' her father shouted out in rage. His shout fell on deaf ears as her mother had already started the engine which sent another pile of leaves up in the air. He flung his rake down in temper and went off into the house for a cup of coffee.

'You know we have to pick up Poppy's friend Sarah on the way and drop them both off at the archery club before 11am.'

'I don't know why she wants to learn to shoot, are they going to play cowboys and Indians in the woods?' Lily asked scornfully.

'Why are you being so hateful? I didn't sneer when you went for your audition and for the last two weeks we have had to listen to you going on about your little witch part for breakfast, dinner and tea. I'm sick of it.'

'That's enough girls,' their mother said.

They travelled in silence; the weather seemed to

change to match their mood. The sky darkened and it started to rain heavily so that when they reached Sarah's she had to run out to the car under an enormous umbrella held by her father.

In Leiston the two younger girls were dropped off at the archery club. Lily was given the money for the costume material and headed off to the haberdashery shop whilst her mother went to the library.

It didn't take Lily long to select a black taffeta material which had a greenish shine when held to the light. The assistant measured out the require amount, folded it up and wrapped it in brown paper tied around with string. Lily paid and left the shop with the parcel hugged to her chest not looking where she was going.

'Well, well, if it isn't the school's witch, careful boys, she might put a spell on us,' said Jed Briggs as he blocked Lily's way out of the shop door.

He grabbed her parcel and started to throw it between his two friends. Lily ran between the three of them trying to wrestle the material from them.

'Where's your little sister then?' asked Jed with a malicious smile on his face.

'Why do you want to know? Just leave her alone.'

Just then one of Jed's friends dropped the parcel in the middle of a puddle.

In silence they all looked down at the split parcel, black taffeta spilling out into the wet mud.

Lily sobbed in relief as she saw her mother walking towards the group.

'Hey, what are you boys up to?' her mother called out.

'Oh Mum, look what they have done to my nice

costume material.'

'Quick leg it,' said Jed to his friends. 'I'll find your sister later,' he whispered over his shoulder as he ran off with his pals.

Her mother put the soggy parcel into a plastic carrier bag assuring her that the mud would wash out. She looked at Lily's forlorn face and said she would treat her to her favourite lunch in the trendy Pasta 'n' Pizza Bar.

While her mother queued at the counter, Lily felt uneasy wondering what Jed Briggs wanted with Poppy.

If she had known what was on Jed's mind at that very moment, she would have felt very uneasy indeed.

Sarah's mother had collected the girls from archery classes and taken them back to her house. After lunch she suggested they take the dog for a walk. The rain had stopped but the sky was still overcast and the wind whipped up the tops of the tall pine trees that surrounded the cottage. Wrapped up in warm waterproof jackets and feet protected from the damp undergrowth by wearing Wellingtons the girls and Rex the dog set off through the woods. Sarah knew the tracks like the back of her hand as she often accompanied her father who was the woodsman for the National Trust land.

Poppy was relieved to hear that Sarah's home was actually nearer the beach than her own. The 's' bend shaped coast line meant that Poppy's part of the beach couldn't be seen from the stretch of beach that Sarah used.

It was hardly a track they followed, just one that Sarah's family used as a short cut, the tall bracken sprayed rain drops over them as Rex pushed his way along sniffing for rabbits.

Fifteen minutes later they arrived in a grassy clearing riddled with rabbit holes, Rex tore around like a mad thing trying his best to dig his way into the holes, scattering sandy earth onto the girl's faces.

'Rex, will you *STOP THAT*!' yelled Poppy wiping sand from her eyes.

She looked up realising they had already reached the beach. The dark grey waves topped with murky white foam crashed upon the shore. Poppy was surprised to see that a lighthouse stood on a rocky headland further along the beach. Its tall red and white striped column was topped by an enormous glass lantern whose beam reached far out to sea.

'*Ooh*, I didn't know that was here, I bet it would be great to live in,' said Poppy.

'It's a lot of steps to go down before you begin your journey to school though. You'll have to ask horrid Jed Briggs what it's like, he lives there. His dad's the lighthouse keeper,' said Sarah.

'Really – let's go and have a look at it, the tides on the turn, by the time we reach it we will be able to climb on the surrounding rocks.'

They found it hard going over the pebbles in Wellingtons, especially as Rex ran around their ankles waiting for sticks to be thrown into the sea for him to retrieve. As they grew nearer, Poppy noticed two figures talking on the causeway to the lighthouse. One was wearing a bright green cloak.

'Oh no, it *can't be*,' said Poppy.

'What's wrong?' asked Sarah.

'Look, it's Mrs. Beddows, the witch, talking to Jed Briggs.'

Sarah was stooping to pick up Rex's stick but when stood up and looked over towards the lighthouse she only saw Jed.

'I can see Jed but no-one else,' said Sarah.

'Where on earth did she go to?'

'Well, she's not on the beach and she didn't have time to climb the steps to the lighthouse entrance,' replied Sarah.

Jed had seen them approaching and walked towards them,

'Poppy isn't it? Just the person I wanted to see,' he said in what he thought was a friendly voice.

Poppy remembered how nasty he had been to Lily at the auditions for the school's play and didn't trust the smile on his face. She scowled at him.

'I believe you have something that belongs to a friend of mine, give it back and I'll let you go home without thumping you one,' he said menacingly.

'You leave her alone, you're nothing but a bully if you think you can hit girls younger than yourself!' shouted Sarah pushing her face up to his.

Jed pushed Sarah to the ground and then things really started to hot up. Poppy ran at Jed and pummelled him in the chest; he then gave her a hard shove causing her to knock over poor Sarah just as she was getting to her feet again. Sarah fell against Poppy and both girls landed on their bottoms, the water lapping over their legs. Rex barked loudly, jumping at Jed's back, which made him topple into the water, face down. Rex then tore Jed's trousers as he bit his bottom trying to shake him like a rag doll. Jed soaked to the skin and with seaweed tangled in his hair struggled to his feet.

'You'll both pay for this,' he shouted as he ran up the steps to the lighthouse, hands over the tear trying to hide his bare bottom.

They roared with laughter as they watched him go but then realised the sorry state that they were in themselves and laughed so much that tears ran down their faces. Rex joined in by licking first Sarah's and then Poppy's face which hampered them getting to their feet.

They took off their Wellingtons which were full of water and their soaking wet jeans. It was lucky that only the bottom of their jackets were wet so their bodies kept warm but the wind whipped cruelly around their cold legs as they ran quickly back towards the woods.

The sky darkened and rain threatened, as barefooted, they picked their way carefully through the woods.

'What was that?' asked Poppy.

'What was what?'

'I thought I heard someone call,' said Poppy.

'It's just the wind and your imagination, don't worry, not far to go now.'

But Poppy knew that she had heard her name being called softly in the high swaying pine trees.

She sighed with relief when Sarah's home came into view, the chimney smoking a warm welcome to them both.

5

Lily and Poppy set off for school a bit earlier Monday morning. Lily had suggested calling for Sarah after hearing about their encounter with Jed.

Sarah wheeled her cycle out of the gate and saw Poppy and Lily waiting for her. 'Oh, you can't think how pleased I am to see you both. I've been a bit worried as Jed cycles the same way to school as me.'

'It was Lily's idea, she said there's safety in numbers and it's not that much out of our way.'

Sarah smiled at Lily as they cycled off down the lane. Lily told them she wanted to be early so that they had time to tell Toby and Melanie what Jed had been up to over the weekend.

When they reached the school, they put their cycles in the almost empty racks and looked around for Toby and Melanie.

'There they are,' said Sarah pointing to the far corner of the playground. She hung back when Poppy and Lily started to walk towards them. Lily turned and said, 'Come on Sarah, you're in on this too now after your skirmish with Jed and you haven't heard what happened to me in Leiston yet.'

Sarah's face lit up, Poppy took her arm and the two of them skipped after Lily to where their friends were sitting under a tree reading their scripts.

Toby and Melanie were angry when they heard what happened to Lily's material at the hands of Jed and his friends and when Poppy and Sarah told their story Toby became even more angry.

'I'll sort him out after school tonight,' he said.

'No don't do that, we've had our revenge,' said Poppy as she explained what had happened to Jed after Rex had bitten his bottom.

Their laughter could still be heard over the noise of the rapidly filling playground and when they saw Jed putting his bike in the rack Toby cheekily called out,

'You OK Jed, you look a bit saddle sore to me.'

This started them off in fits of laughter again. Jed, red in the face came towards them and said menacingly,

'Mark my words, you lot will pay for this one way or another.'

Just then the bell sounded and they followed Jed towards the double doors to join the queue.

'He does sound angry. We'll have to be on our guard, he's bound to get even with us,' said Melanie.

'I think Jed will try to ambush us individually. I said to Sarah this morning that there is safety in numbers, so we must stick together as much as possible,' said Lily.

'You're a newcomer Lily, you don't know how ruthless Jed can be,' said Toby as they filed into school, agreeing to meet in the hall after lessons.

Sarah said she was happy to watch with Poppy so that they could cycle home together.

They didn't know then just how soon Jed's campaign of revenge would begin.

Lessons passed uneventfully during the morning for the older three children as Jed was a model pupil and didn't antagonise Lily once. Lunchtime they found a quiet corner and practiced their lines for the evening rehearsal, again Jed was ominously quiet and kept his distance from them.

Classes split for the last two periods in the afternoon. The boys had a football match on the school playing field, whilst the girls had domestic science.

After the heavy rain over the weekend the pitch was soggy underfoot but these conditions didn't mar Toby's enjoyment of the game. Acting was great fun but secretly Toby had ambitions to be a footballer.

The pitch soon became a quagmire from the onslaught of twenty-two pairs of robust boy's feet and Toby had a job to maintain his balance.

The coach put the whistle to his mouth ready to signal end of lessons, Toby was in the process of kicking the ball from his opponents foot when Jed ran up to join the tackle and purposefully knocked Toby to the ground. The whistle went but Jed jumped on Toby and rolled him over and pushed his face down in the mud.

'Stop that you two, get off to the showers before I give you both detention,' shouted the coach.

Toby wiped the mud out of his eyes as he got to his feet, bending over to get his breath, he heard Jed laughing as he ran across the field back to the gym. The showers were all occupied when Toby reached the locker room and he had to wait his turn. He felt in his blazer pocket which hung on his peg for his watch and realised he would have to get a move on if he were to make rehearsals on time. Most of the boys showered quickly but Toby when his turn came had a job to get the mud out of his hair, ears and even his nose.

Clean at last, he turned the shower off and noticed how quiet the steam filled room had become. He was on his own with only the monotonous drips from the shower-heads to break the eerie silence. Dressing quickly, he shoved his dirty kit in his school bag. The main locker room door held fast when he tried to open it. He pulled, shook and finally kicked the door but it wouldn't budge, realising he was locked in he tried shouting but no-one answered his calls. He was already late rehearsals.

*

Lily and Melanie had stowed the cakes they had made in the panniers on their bikes and with Poppy and Sarah were now waiting in the hall for Toby. When Miss Wells arrived followed closely by a smirking Jed but no Toby they began to wonder what had happened to him.

Miss Wells called for everyone to take their places for the scene they were to rehearse when she realised Toby was missing.

'Where's Toby, Melanie?'

'I don't know, he said he would meet us here after lessons. He wouldn't want to miss rehearsals; I can't think what's keeping him.'

'If he can't be here on time I'll have to think about giving his part to someone else. Jed you can step in for the moment.'

Melanie groaned as Jed took to the stage, grinning at her like a Cheshire cat as he started to recite Toby's lines. Miss Wells had to correct Jed several times and after a frustrating ten minutes she was relieved when the door opened and Toby burst in out of breath and covered in dust.

'No excuses now,' she said telling him to take his place and for Jed to resume his own part.

'Didn't work, did it?' Toby whispered. Jed looked furious as he returned to his own position on stage.

Melanie and Lily raised questioning eyebrows at Toby who was only able to mouth that he would tell them later.

Rehearsals came to an end.

'Why on earth were you late?' Melanie asked Toby. 'Miss Wells was so annoyed she would have given your part to Jed for good if you hadn't turned up when you did.'

'It's Jed's fault I was late, his revenge started earlier than we thought. He told them of his tackle with Jed in the mud.

'It took me ages to get clean, I was last to shower and then found I was locked in. It was obviously Jed's work. It took me a good ten minutes to escape; I was able to get out by climbing upon a toilet cistern and heaving myself through the small opened window. I've ended up being nearly as dirty as I was after the football match.

'You're right when you said Jed's ruthless, it proves he can still get at us even when we think we are safe amongst our school friends,' said Lily.

'Let's forget about Jed for the minute, how did you think the rehearsals went?' Melanie asked Poppy and Sarah.

Jed forgotten, they noisily discussed the play as they wheeled their bikes out of the school gates.

Saying goodnight to Toby and Melanie, Lily and the two youngsters cycled off.

Leaving Sarah safely at her gate, it was almost dark by the time they turned into their drive. Poppy jumped when the black cat jumped out in front of them spitting and hissing angrily.

'Who does that ugly cat belong to and why does it always hang around our garden, it's not as if we encourage it?' said Lily.

Poppy had an idea about the cat but thought Lily would laugh if she told her. Instead she said,

'What with witches, exciting plays and nasty goings on with Jed do you still think that Suffolk is more boring than our quiet life in London?'

'No, I must admit that I am enjoying our life here but I think you can forget about having witches for neighbours. The only witch you'll encounter is me when I'm dressed up in my costume for 'Mac the knife,' laughed Lily.

They wheeled their bikes round to the shed.

Poppy thought to herself that in spite of what Lily said they hadn't seen the last of Mrs. Beddows yet.

6

Lily was kept so busy over the next few weeks with rehearsals after school and fittings for her costume which her mother was making that she had no time to wonder what had become of Mrs. Beddows.

Poppy wondered though, it stood to reason that if Mrs. Beddows wasn't in fact a witch then she must live somewhere in the area so she decided to ask Miss Meredith to help track her down.

One Saturday afternoon as Lily and her mother were bent over their sewing Poppy said she was off to visit Miss Meredith. Lily showed no surprise at this visit and her mother's response was, 'not to be late for dinner.'

Miss Meredith answered the knock at her door and welcomed Poppy with a smile into the dark interior of the lounge. After sinking into a large comfy settee Poppy explained the reason for her visit. Miss Meredith turned on her computer and accessed the Census records, no matter how far back they looked no trace could be found of a Naomi Beddows living in or around their area of Suffolk.

'Does that mean she really is a witch?' Poppy asked.

'It's hard to believe I know. Her name's on those books in the attic so she must have been a real person. She doesn't seem to exist now, though, so when did she live? That's one question that even *I* can't answer.'

Poppy shivered as Miss Meredith turned on the lamps and said,

'It's getting dark, I'll walk you home.'

They said goodnight at the gates to Poppy's home. Lights shone in the kitchen, throwing her mother's silhouette onto the pulled down blind as she served their dinner.

It was now very dark; the large oak trees bordering the garden had already shed their leaves, their barren branches reached towards Poppy like gross talons.

She walked quickly towards the house trying to keep her eyes off the trees but when a bat flew close by her head she let out an almighty scream and ran hell bent for leather towards the house.

'There you are! Your father was just coming to look for you, wash your hands, I'm just dishing up,' her mother said all in one breath.

When the family were all seated around the table Lily said,

'Sarah telephoned; she sounded quite excited but wouldn't tell me why. You're to phone her as soon as you can.'

Poppy went to get up but one look from her father made her sit down again.

They hurried though their dinner and when their parents took their coffee through to the lounge, they washed and wiped up in record time.

When Poppy rang, Sarah answered the phone herself.

'I've been waiting for you to ring for ages. You remember that day on the beach you said you saw Mrs. Beddows talking to Jed by the lighthouse but I didn't. Well I did today!

I took Rex to throw sticks in the sea and there they both were. She's tall and thin with silver spikey hair and wears a bright green cape doesn't she?'

'Yes, that's her, you *really* saw her too? I had started to think I had imagined her,' said Poppy in relief.

'She seemed real enough to me, to Jed too I should think, he was deep in conversation with her and kept nodding his head to whatever it was she was saying.'

Poppy went on to tell Sarah of her visit to Miss Meredith and the outcome of their search on the internet.

'Oh, that's what you've been doing, you might have asked me along' said Lily peevishly. Poppy turned to her and said,

'All you want to do is talk about the play and your costume.'

'Hello, are you there Poppy?

Poppy had covered the mouthpiece of the telephone whilst she had been talking to Lily.

'Sorry Sarah, Lily was grousing as I hadn't included her in my search for Mrs. Beddows. Anyway we can discuss it at church tomorrow after the harvest festival service, bye for now.'

The family usually walked to church on Sunday. This was the only time of the week that they were able to do something altogether since Poppy had joined the archery classes and Lily had become involved in the school play.

Today however, their parents took the car as it was needed to transport the produce for the harvest festival. Poppy and Lily decided to walk as it was such a beautiful autumn morning. Leaves in shades of red, yellow and brown blew along the ground in the slight wind and the sun was promising to break through the early morning mist before lunchtime.

The interior of the church was decked out in garlands of hedgerow flowers. A nature table had been produced by the young children from the Sunday school. Leaves, feathers and wilted wild flowers lay next to shiny brown conkers displayed beside their green spiky cases.

The vicar kept the sermon short and after the final hymn of *All things bright and beautiful,* the children queued up before the altar to lay their gifts. Lily gave the cake she had made at school; mum's chutney was added to jams and preserves made by other local housewives. Their father was pleased to make an offering from his own vegetable patch, even though they were already growing in the garden when they moved into the house.

Service over, everyone filed out, shaking the vicar's hand as they left. Sarah turned to Lily and Poppy and whispered,

'Look who's over there, I didn't think he was a church goer.'

They were just in time to see Jed disappear around the back of the church.

'I bet he's up to no good, let's see what he's doing,' said Lily.

Leaving the parents talking to the vicar, they followed Jed. They peered cautiously around a buttress on the corner of the building but Jed was nowhere to be seen.

Returning to the porch to say goodbye to the vicar, they were amazed when Jed walked out of the door as bold as brass.

He smirked, doffed an imaginary cap and said,

'Morning girls, lovely day,' and then swaggered out through the lynch-gate into the lane.

'Of all the cheek,' said Poppy.

'When we see Toby and Melanie at school tomorrow I think we'll suggest that we take it in turns to spy on Jed. He's up to no good I'm sure,' said Lily.

'We'll call for you as usual in the morning,' said Poppy as Sarah set off down the lane accompanied by her parents. Poppy and Lily walked home at a brisk pace, eager for their harvest Sunday lunch.

7

Monday morning the five friends were huddled in their usual corner of the playground putting forward theories as to what Jed had been up to in the church. Melanie looked thoughtful and said,

'Bearing in mind Poppy's finding of the silver key and the sudden appearance on the scene of Mrs. Beddows and her meeting with Jed on the beach, the only conclusion that I can come to, is that Mrs. B wants Jed to try to get the book out of the church and get the key off of Poppy.'

'I should have thought of that but I've been so taken up with my part in the play that I've ignored Poppy's attempts to convince me Mrs. Beddows is evil,' said an ashamed Lily.

'Well who can blame you, who believes in witches these days,' said Toby.

'On Sunday, I reckon Jed was casing the joint as they say in the films,' said Sarah.

Hearing footsteps, they looked up and said good morning when they saw Miss Meredith approaching. Looking at Poppy she said,

'After your visit I decided to look more thoroughly through those old books in my attic. A very old one with a faded cover was obviously a child's book. On the flyleaf, was written, to Naomi on her 8th birthday, 31st

October 1773. What do you think to that Poppy?' Miss Meredith asked.

'That it proves what I've been trying to tell them all along, that Mrs. Beddows really is a witch. She couldn't possibly have lived in 1773 and still be around today,' declared a jubilant Poppy.

'Have you noticed another thing, her birthday's 31st October' said Toby.

'What's so unusual about that?' Melanie asked.

'Halloween,' shouted the other four and Miss Meredith together.

The teacher hurried off into school after asking them to keep her in touch with developments. Lily just had time to tell Toby and Melanie of her plan for spying on Jed before the school bell went. They both agreed it would be a good idea as they joined the queue of jostling youngsters pushing their way through the double doors into the warm.

Lily and Poppy were surprised to see a police car outside the church as they cycled passed Tuesday morning. They could see two uniformed constables searching amongst the gravestones.

'Goodness, do you reckon Jed has stolen the book of spells?' Lily asked.

They stopped, propped their bikes against the churchyard wall but were barred from entering the lynch-gate by a non-uniformed man.

'What can I do for you young ladies?' he asked smiling.

'I don't suppose you two know anything about this break-in do you?'

They shook their heads but Lily asked what was taken. The inspector said that he wasn't at liberty to say and that they had better run along to school.

Sarah, waiting at her gate, couldn't understand what they were trying to say as they cycled towards her. Both were shouting to her at the same time. Finally Lily gave in and let Poppy tell her friend about the break-in.

Cycling as fast as they could so that there was time to talk to Toby and Melanie, they were overtaken by Jed as they neared the school.

'You been a naughty boy then Jed, we've just had a word with the police at the church,' shouted Lily.

'Keep your nose out or you'll get a punch on it if you're not careful,' he replied nastily.

'You don't know who you are dealing with and I'm not referring to us,' Lily said.

'I don't like you Jed,' said Poppy, 'but that woman's *evil*, she's a witch and I wouldn't like to see you disappear if she gets her hands on her spell book.'

'Don't be daft kid, she's just an old woman who's prepared to pay well to get her own property back,' Jed said in a scoffing voice.

'Don't say you haven't been warned,' shouted Lily as Jed turned into the school yard.

Toby and Melanie heard Lily's shout as they were putting their bikes into the racks. Toby asked what she was warning Jed about and she explained as the three girls put their bikes besides the others.

'If Jed has stolen the book we really will have to

40

follow his every move to find out where he's hidden it,' said Melanie.

'He wouldn't risk hiding it at the lighthouse in case his father found it,' said Sarah.

They agreed that Lily, Poppy and Sarah would follow him home from school after rehearsals and Toby and Melanie would keep watch on the lighthouse at the weekend and would call Lily on her mobile if they saw Jed do anything suspicious.

'Of course, there will probably be an account of the break-in in the mornings newspaper,' said Lily.

'We should know for certain whether the books been stolen then,' she continued.

They all agreed that as Jed would now be on his guard it was imperative that they started there spying that very afternoon.

'These morning discussions are getting to be a regular thing,' said Toby as they joined the queue as the bell went.

8

Wednesday morning's paper bought headline news of the break-in. Lily and Poppy tried to read over their father's shoulder until he declared he was taking his paper and coffee into the lounge to read in peace whilst his daughters were told to get on with their breakfast.

He was still reading his paper as they reluctantly left the house for school.

Sarah wasn't able to add to their knowledge as her father had taken his paper with him. She told them that her father had a hut deep in the wood with a comfy chair in which he sat for his elevenses whilst he read his paper.

'Oh well, perhaps Toby or Melanie will know more,' Lily said as they cycled towards school.

Their friends were already in the corner of the playground and they could see that both were absorbed in the newspaper in Toby's hands.

Rushing up to them, Poppy said,

'Does it say what was stolen; does it mention the silver book?'

Toby shook his head and said,

'Listen to this...

Inspector Perry of the Suffolk Constabulary confirmed that St. Augustus church in the small hamlet of Redham was broken into sometime Sunday evening.

A very sturdy oak cupboard had been broken open, possibly with the use of a chisel that was left at the scene. This cupboard housed the parish records which seemed to be intact.

The reporter went on to say that the vicar seemed very embarrassed when ask what was missing and said that as far as he could see all records seemed to be in place.'

'Of course he wouldn't admit to having a witches' spell book in the church would he?' Melanie answered.

'If the book has gone, he didn't actually tell a lie, he just said that the records seemed to be all there,' said Poppy loyally.

'As agreed we followed Jed home last night and kept him in sight until he reached the lighthouse. We couldn't hang around though as it was beginning to get dark so we cycled back with Sarah and then went home,' Lily told Toby and Melanie.

Rehearsals went well every night for the rest of the week, performances were more polished. Jed even improved, reading his lines without mistake but lacking the passion of Toby's acting. He gave the five friends a wide berth after Lily's remarks about the police.

Each night the three girls followed Jed at a distance and each night he arrived home without stopping off on the way. By the time they left Sarah at her home Friday evening, they were glad that Toby and Melanie would be taking over the watch on the Saturday as it had been such a boring exercise.

But things were about to change tomorrow!

9

Sarah's mother pulled up on her drive Saturday morning after returning the girls from their archery class. Sarah and Poppy struggled to unload their equipment as their bows and arrows kept tangling together. Rex barked a welcome, knowing a walk might come later. Startled pigeons flew out of the woods, Poppy and Sarah turned in time to see Jed leave the lane outside the cottage and take the track which led deep into the forest.

'*Quick* let's follow him,' said Sarah.

'Oh no you don't; lunch first you've had a busy morning and need to replace your energy levels before you go traipsing in the woods,' Sarah's mother said.

They pulled a face as they entered the kitchen but willingly laid the table whilst they waited for a large pot of stew to heat upon the stove.

Sarah's mother raised her eyes and sighed as she watched them eat as quickly as they could. They asked if they could be excused washing up as they wanted to take Rex for a walk. Sarah's mother saw through this excuse but agreed nevertheless.

Grabbing their coats and Rex's lead they dashed off along the track into the heart of the wood.

It was easy to follow Jed's trail by the broken bracken which overhung the track and by the way Rex stopped and sniffed the ground and then ran on every so often.

'Rex has picked up Jed's scent; it looks as if he's heading towards Dad's hut,' said Sarah.

When they reached the clearing there was no sign of Jed but Sarah noticed that the pile of logs stacked at the side of the hut had been moved.

'He must have hidden the book under those logs. We're too late, we'll never catch up with him now,' she said.

'I bet he's gone to hand it over to Mrs. Beddows and collect his money. Every time we see them together it's by the lighthouse, quick let's make for the beach now,' said Poppy excitedly.

They had reached what Sarah referred to as the rabbit clearing when Rex let out an agonizing howl. He was rooted to the spot staring at someone who was half hidden, standing behind a tree.

'What on earth's wrong with Rex, I've never seen him act like this before?' said Sarah.

Both went deathly white as Mrs. Beddows stepped onto the path in front of them. Rex whined, turned tail and fled towards home.

'Hello, Poppy, just the girl I wanted to see. That's a pretty little necklace you have there,' said Mrs. Beddows as she advanced towards her.

Poppy's hand went to her throat where the key hung on its dainty chain but Mrs. Beddows was too quick for her. She grabbed Poppy in a vice like grip and snapped the chain from around her neck. Poor Poppy yelled in pain as the chain bit into her skin.

Sarah rushed to comfort her friend, dabbing her hanky to Poppy's neck to stop the flow of blood. When they finally looked up Mrs. Beddows had vanished into thin air.

'Quickly, down to the beach,' said Poppy as she ran with a frightened Sarah following on her heels.

*

Unbeknown to the younger girls, Toby, Melanie and Lily were also on the trail of Jed.

Toby and Melanie had set out early that morning to keep watch on the lighthouse. They hid their bikes in the sand dunes and lay on their stomachs peering through the grass waiting for Jed to appear on the causeway.

The tide was out and the beach empty, only the screech of overhead seagulls and the whisper of the waving grasses could be heard by the hidden observers. It was almost noon and Melanie was on the point of dozing off when Toby nudged her in the ribs, Jed was making off across the beach towards the lane.

Toby rang Lily on his mobile and told her where Jed was headed.

'Can you watch out for him from Sarah's home and follow him if possible. We'll keep a safe distance behind him. Put your mobile on silent mode and we can text each other if he does actually go to retrieve the book. My bet is that he's hidden it somewhere in the wood, bye for now.'

Lily got out her bike and peddled for all she was worth along the lanes to Sarah's. Jed was just crossing the plank bridge over the stream into the wood. She saw the car in the drive but daren't knock for Poppy and Sarah as she might lose sight of Jed. Instead she laid her bike against the cottage fence and went after Jed as quietly as possible.

Unlike Sarah and Poppy, Lily wasn't familiar with the track and had no idea where it led. Jed wasn't troubling to move quietly so Lily found it easy to keep track of him.

When all went quiet she stopped behind a large tree and texted Toby, giving her position. There was no reply but she heard rustling in the undergrowth and was relieved to see Melanie and Toby approaching, Toby with finger to lips for quiet.

The sound of falling logs filled the air, the three friends crept forward and hidden by a group of large trees were able to watch whilst Jed pulled a large dirty sack from out of the log pile. They nearly gave themselves away laughing as he fell back on his bottom in the wet earth.

Stalking him quietly from tree to tree in the hope of catching him red-handed giving the book to Mrs. Beddows, they were amazed to find themselves at the beach.

'This way through the woods is much shorter, why on earth did he come the long way down the lane?' asked Melanie.

'Someone might have seen him enter the woods from the beach, going down the lane he could be going anywhere, he returned this way as there was less chance of anyone noticing him carrying a heavy sack,' said Toby.

'We had better wait a bit and then walk casually

along the beach in case he turns around and notices us,' said Lily.

Walking slowly they stopped to pick up shells and bits of driftwood but keeping a wary eye on Jed all the time. When almost at the lighthouse they were stopped in their tracks by the most blood curdling howl they had ever heard coming from the direction of the woods.

10

The tide was on the turn, waves were beginning to cover the rocks on the peninsular that the lighthouse stood upon. The causeway was just above water as Jed stepped onto it, hearing the horrible howl, he turned and looked back towards the woods but to his dismay saw his class mates closing in on him.

Just then Poppy and Sarah ran out onto the beach, seeing the others Poppy called out,

'Stop Jed, he's got the silver spell book.'

'We know,' Lily called back.

'You don't know that Mrs. Beddows has just snatched the silver key from me, we must stop them meeting,' yelled Poppy.

'*Quick, after him,*' shouted Toby as he sprinted across the sand.

Jed slammed the door in Toby's face but he didn't have time to lock it. The three older children climbed the winding steps, higher and higher. Toby with all his football practice went up quicker than Melanie and Lily who had to stop every so often to get their breath. Toby couldn't match Jed's pace, after all he went up and down these steps regularly every day.

Poppy and Sarah ran across the beach. Sarah stumbled and Poppy bent down to help her up and were just in time to see a flash of bright green disappear through the lighthouse door.

'Where on earth has she sprung from, the beach was deserted except for us lot?' said Poppy.

'I don't like it,' whispered Sarah looking really scared.

'Come on we have to follow her, what can she do with all the others there too?

Sarah hung back but Poppy grabbed her hand and pulled her towards the causeway which was slowly being covered by water.

They rubbed the soles of their trainers dry on a coconut doormat before trying to climb the steps. It was hard going for the two youngsters, their legs not so strong or long as the older children's.

Jed had pushed the door to the platform around the outside of the beacon shut. He then pulled a box behind the door to try to stop Toby getting in. It was a waste of time, Toby gave one almighty kick and the door burst open pushing the box back with it.

'Keep back or I'll throw this book over the side,' said Jed as he held up the heavy sack with both hands, his back against the railings.

'What, and have the witch turn you into a bigger toad than you already are,' said Toby in a serious voice.

'You lot keep talking a lot of rot about witches, this is the twenty-first century you know,' scoffed Jed.

Toby realised he was still carrying a piece of driftwood in his hands from the beach. He threw it at Jed and caught him on the knees which made him fall to the ground, sack and book with him.

The two struggled, Toby got hold of the sack when a voice as hard as steel said,

'I think that belongs to ME.'

Mrs. Beddows stood in the doorway, chain and key dangling in one hand. She advanced towards the boys, her bony claw like hand reaching towards the sack. Lily burst onto the platform followed closely by Melanie. Lily reacted quickly by grabbing the key as the woman bent to pick up the sack.

'RUN LILY,' called Toby.

Just then Poppy's voice was heard calling breathlessly from lower down the steps.

'The witch is here somewhere ... she's got my key ... you must get it back ...'

Mrs. Beddows' face went purple.

'That WRETCHED guardian of the key, she SHAN'T have it back.'

And with that she let out a horrendous screech; then lunged towards Lily who had run around the large lantern platform. Poppy and Sarah were just in time to see her charge at Lily. Mrs. Beddows turned slightly when Poppy called out,

'Where's my key?'

Lily stepped to one side and Mrs. Beddows went crashing through the weak iron railings down onto the rocks below.

For one moment the children stood in shock before running to look carefully over the railings.

'But she's not there,' said Melanie in amazement.

The others couldn't believe their eyes either.

Jed was still on the floor shaking visibly but even he felt compelled to get up and look over the railings.

The foaming waves which crashed over the partially exposed rocks were a peculiar sulphur yellow and bright green. There was no sight of Mrs. Beddows nor the intricately carved silver book.

Hearing barking and people shouting they ran around to the causeway side of the lighthouse to see Sarah's mother and father standing with Jed's father. They were all shouting and Rex tore around their legs barking.

Sarah made out that her father was asking if they were all ok and shouted back that they were.

The sea had completely covered the causeway by now and they realised they would have to wait until the tide turned to get off the lighthouse.

'Come on Jed, lead the way to your kitchen, I think we can all do with a hot drink,' said Toby.

Jed let himself be led down the steps and into the living quarters but it was left to Lily and Melanie to make the drinks, Jed was still in shock.

'Oh, I've just realised my key has gone into the sea with Mrs. Beddows,' said Poppy.

'No it hasn't,' said Lily as she took it out of her pocket.

Poppy hugged her sister.

'Well I still can't understand where she's gone, she should be laying on the rocks, injured if not dead,' said Melanie.

Poppy just had to have the last word.

'Salt water, it's a known fact that witches can't live in salt water, it makes them dissolve. I said all along that she was a witch, didn't I?

11

Weeks of rehearsals over, it was the last day of term and now for the real thing.

Poppy and Sarah stood by the doors of the rapidly filling hall taking the tickets for 'Mac the knife,' a modern version of Shakespere's play *Macbeth*.

With the exception of Jed they had all recovered fairly quickly from their experience with Mrs. Beddows at the lighthouse.

On that day as the tide went out Sarah's parents had followed Jed's father up the spiral staircase, hampered by a very wet Rex who rushed passed them barking madly.

Poppy and Lily's parents had arrived in answer to Lily's telephone call soon after.

Pandemonium broke loose as everyone tried to talk at once, except for Jed who sat on a chair staring into the fire with a glazed expression in his eyes.

None of the grown-ups had ever met Mrs. Beddows so it was no wonder they had difficulty in believing the story of a dissolving witch. Jed's father thought the story was to cover up the fact that one of them must have been playing about and broken the railings.

They returned to school on Monday and decided not to tell anyone else about Mrs. Beddows. If their own parents didn't believe them, their school mates certainly wouldn't, they would only be branded, barking mad.

Jed was off school for two weeks. When Miss Wells said she would have to replace him in the play, Toby said he would visit Jed and help him with his lines at home.

Jed was relieved when Toby said he would coach him and the two became firm friends as they learnt their lines together over the next few weeks.

When Lily, Melanie, Poppy and Sarah visited him he had the grace to look very ashamed as he apologised for all he had done.

It was agreed that his past deeds together with Mrs. Beddows should be forgotten and never spoken of again.

The hall was almost full as the vicar and his wife handed their tickets to Poppy who indicated the saved seats in the first row beside Sarah's and her own parents.

As the lights dimmed they took their own seats besides Miss Meredith.

Miss Wells came out between the curtains to introduce the play they had watched many times.

Tonight however, with colourful and authentic costumes, imaginative scenery and atmospheric lighting they almost felt transported back to another age.

Lily and Melanie gave a good account of themselves but Toby stole the scene as he recited:

Is this a dagger which I see before me,
The handle towards my hand,
Come let me clutch thee,
I have thee not, and yet I see thee still.

Melanie's heart swelled with pride as he continued his speech and Jed's father clapped his son's performance as hard as any parent at the end of the play.

When the lights went up an excited Poppy turned to Sarah and said,

'That was great. I've decided I'm going to be a playwright when I grow up. What do you think my first play will be called?

'I don't know, what?'

'The Guardian of the Key.'

Author's note

The black cat? Strangely, that disappeared and was never seen again from the day Mrs. Beddows fell off the lighthouse.

The Southwold Adventure

1

'For goodness sake, slow down,' said Poppy as she stopped her bike on the iron Bailey bridge.

Her friend Sarah, pulled up beside her and said breathlessly,

'It's alright for you older three; you have longer, stronger legs and can go faster than me and Poppy.'

Poppy's sister Lily pulled a face, looked at her friends and said,

'You thought this trip by bike would be too much for them Melanie and you've been proved right.'

'Well we are here now so don't let's moan,' said Toby. 'Poppy and Sarah have done really well and I think they deserve an ice-cream in the Chandlery; my treat.'

Poppy smiled at Toby sweetly, he was her hero.

The five cycled over the noisy bridge to the Southwold side of the river Blyth. Boats of all shapes and sizes were tied up at moorings outside the Harbour Inn and Sailing Club, whilst on the verges beside the pot holed unmade road, boats in various stages of repair awaited their owner's attention.

Squalling seagulls circled overhead as the fishermen unloaded their catch. The fish would be sold from the rickety wooden shacks which lined the river bank.

Poppy and Sarah wobbled a bit as they tried to manoeuvre around the pot holes without falling off their bikes. Reaching the Chandlery, they lent their bikes against the wooden walls, climbed the steps and entered the building. Nets, ropes and many other sea faring articles were displayed for sale. Part of the building had been turned into a tea room cum ice-cream parlour. The different varieties of ice-cream left the children spoilt for choice.

The girls sat on a bench outside licking the dripping cones and keeping an eye on the seagulls which dived rather close to their heads. Toby was on the riverbank admiring a fishing boat.

'I like her name,' he said as the girls came closer. 'It's called *An ill wind.*'

He was trying to peer into the portholes when an angry looking fisherman approached, shaking his fist at them.

'Hey, you kids, clear out, that's private property.'

Sarah and Poppy were quite scared when he marched straight up to Toby, and pulled him roughly by the arm away from the boat.

'*YOU CAN'T DO THAT!*' yelled Melanie fiercely.

'Leave it girls, come on let's get out of here, we don't want to look at his rusty old wreck anyway.'

The man scowled at them but kept his eye on them until they got back on their bikes and rode away.

'I hoped we were going to have an exciting holiday but I didn't expect it to start quite like this,' said Lily.

'Don't let's worry about that nasty character, it's going to be exciting staying in a caravan for two weeks as well as becoming film stars,' said Melanie.

'Yes, we are lucky that Miss Wells thought of us when her friend wanted children for the film he is shooting here,' said Toby.

'I expect she recommended you after your brilliant performance in the school play last year,' said Melanie proudly.*

'I know me and Lily gave a good account of ourselves, but it was you who stole the show.' *(see Guardian of the Key)*

'What about us?' piped up Sarah. 'We took the tickets on the door on the night.'

The others all laughed at the look on her eager young face.

'Well we all have parts this time, however small they may be and it's a good way to spend the summer holidays,' said Toby.

'I know, let' go and have a look around the fairground,' he continued.

'If it's open we can have some rides,' said Poppy.

'Oh yes, just after we have eaten these rich ices,' Lily said sarcastically.

'I'd like to see the fairground where the film's to be set before we meet the director,' said Poppy.

'Come on then, let's go to the caravan first, we can unload our bikes,' said Toby.

The girls followed Toby along the hazardous road to the caravan site. It didn't take them long to find the caravan. Toby unlocked the door and they dumped their panniers on the floor.

'It was really good of Miss Wells to let us have the use of her caravan, not many teachers would trust their pupils that much,' said Melanie.

'She got to know us all pretty well when we joined the drama club,' replied Toby.

'Right, let's go or we won't have time to look around the fairground,' he said as he locked the caravan door. They followed Toby in single file out of the camp site, cycling along Ferry Road towards the fair on the common.

'Look, a crabbing competition at Walberswick. I wouldn't mind entering that,' said Lily pointing to a telegraph pole which had a brightly painted poster pinned to it.

'That might be fun, let's hope we won't be needed on the film set that day, then we could all enter,' said Toby.

Sarah wasn't really too keen on fishing of any kind but she kept quiet, she didn't want her friends to think she was a spoil sport.

'I can see the fairground,' shouted out Poppy. 'It doesn't look as if it is open though.'

As they drew nearer they saw a notice giving opening times pasted onto the side of one of the lorries.

'The fair doesn't open until 4 p.m. so we will have to come back later if we have the time,' said Toby.

They walked around the ground watching the fair folk getting ready for opening time.

A boy of about fourteen was in charge of the dodgems. He gave Lily and Melanie a cheeky grin and shouted, 'Hope you ladies are coming for a ride on my dodgem cars tonight, I'll make sure you get an extra long go.'

'I wouldn't mind having a go, would you Melanie?' Lily asked.

Poppy taunted,

'I bet you just want to see that boy again.'

Lily blushed and gave her sister a dark look and walked off arm in arm with Melanie, her nose in the air.

'I reckon it's time we had some lunch,' said Toby after they had spent time looking at the various side shows and rides being set up. They all agreed and set off on their bikes to find the nearest fish and chip shop.

2

Meet the Director

Sitting on the benches overlooking the sea, they soon tucked into their chips.

'Mum doesn't really like us having too many,' said Lily as she popped a long, salty, chunky, chip into her mouth.

'Right, time to meet Miss Wells and the director,' Toby said jumping to his feet.

'She said she will be at St. Edmunds Theatre with her friend about two-thirty, so we had better get a move on.'

After licking the salt from their fingers they quickly disposed of the chip bags in a nearby bin and excitedly set off on their bikes again.

St. Edmunds Theatre was easy to find, just a few roads back from the sea front.

They entered the lobby and Toby asked at the ticket office if Miss Wells had arrived.

'Oh yes. She told me to expect five children,' said the attendant pushing her glasses up her nose as she peered at them.

'Come with me, I'll take you through to the hall. Be quiet though because some of the actors are rehearsing,' she told them.

Miss Wells heard the doors open, looked up and waved as she came towards them followed by a very tall, bearded man.

'Hello, it's good to see you all again,' she said.

'This is the producer, Mr. McLeod,' she said introducing the tall man.

'And this is Toby, Melanie, Sarah, Lily and her sister Poppy

'I hope you will all enjoy this experience, we might find we have some budding actors amongst you,' he smiled as he shook each child's hand in turn.

'Now don't worry, there's hardly any script to learn, just an odd line or two and of course the action shots to be filmed as the chase scene unfolds in the fairground.'

Mr. McLeod continued to outline their parts, which they all thought sounded very exciting.

'We have already shot the indoor scenes at the film studios in London but we obviously have to come on location for the outside scenes,' he explained.

Just then raised voices could be heard coming from the stage.

'I tell you I am wearing this necklace on the film set,' said a beautiful blonde women in a very loud voice.

'But Miss Carlton it doesn't go with the clothes you will wear for the outside scenes.' This statement was made by the young girl from the props department.

'I tell you I am wearing it and that is that.' Miss Carlton stamped her foot, turned her back on the girl and stormed up to Mr. McLeod.

'Basil *darling*, that dreadful props girl says I can't wear my beautiful diamond pendant on the film set. I can, can't I?' she begged clinging to his arm.

'No, Juliette. I've told you, we won't be insured if it gets damaged or lost on set,' said Mr. McLeod.

'But *Basil* ...,' Juliette Carlton purred.

'No Juliette that's *final*,' said Basil McLeod turning back to the children.

Juliette Carlton turned on her heels and went back to the stage, a thunderous look on her face.

'Sorry folks, Miss Carlton gets a bit temperamental at times but she is a jolly fine actress. You will meet her and the other actors tomorrow.'

'Don't worry Basil; I'm sure the children will get on with them all. I'm glad I only teach drama to school children and not actresses", said Miss Wells.

Basil McLeod laughed.

'Right, I'll see you children on set at the fairground tomorrow, 9 a.m. sharp OK,' he said as he turned back to the stage to resume rehearsals.

Miss Wells said,

'Come on let's go and have some tea. I know a lovely little tea room that sells lovely gooey cakes.'

The children were soon tucking into cakes and drinking lemonade. It was rather noisy as they were all trying to talk at once. Miss Wells looked at them over the top of her cup of coffee, thinking what nice children they were.

'Did you see that diamond pendant Miss Carlton was wearing?' Melanie asked them.

'I did, it was nearly as big as an egg,' exclaimed Poppy.

'That's a slight exaggeration Poppy but I must admit it was rather large,' said Lily.

'It's not very sensible to wear it on a film set, it

64

should really be in a locked safe whilst she is working,' said Miss Wells.

They all agreed with her and hurriedly crammed the last bits of their cake into their mouth's as Miss Wells rose to leave.

'I hope you will all enjoy your acting experience. I'll pop over to see how you are getting on in a few days. I told your mother's that I would collect and bring over some more food supplies for you.'

'Thank you Miss Wells, that's very kind of you,' replied Toby.

They followed her out of the tea room, thanked her for their tea and walked with her back to her car and waved as she drove off down the road.

'We will have to get up early tomorrow if we are to be on set by 9 a.m.,' said Toby.

'It's really exciting isn't it?' said Sarah. 'Wait until our friends see us on film.'

But it was going to turn out more exciting than any of them imagined!

3

Film Stars!

The waves lapped softly on the shore of the deserted beach and seagulls squawked overhead. Poppy woke up first; the sun was shining on her face through a chink in the curtain. She stood up, stretched and yawned and said,

'Come on girls; don't forget we are filming today.'

'What time is it?' Lily asked as she poked her head out of her sleeping bag.

'7 a.m. We will have to get dressed quickly, we will only have time for cereals for breakfast, we don't want to be late on set,' said Melanie who had already unzipped her sleeping bag and was busy looking for her clothes.

'Sarah, come on wake up sleepy head, we are going to be film stars today,' Poppy shouted.

'What on earth was that?' said Lily as a loud thump was heard coming from under the floor followed by some muffled words the girls couldn't make out.

'It sounds as if Toby has hit his head on the base of the caravan as he struggled to get up,' laughed Melanie.

'It's a shame he has to sleep under the van, it's lucky that the weather's so fine,' said Lily as she helped the two youngsters tidy away their bedding.

Toby put his head through the open door and asked if breakfast was ready.

'Goodness Toby, look at your hair, you look like a scarecrow,' laughed Sarah who was having her long hair plaited by Melanie.

'Hey, young Sarah, you wouldn't be laughing if you sat up in bed, forgetting where you were and received an almighty bump on the head,' Toby said but with a smile on his face.

'I don't think I can last the morning on a bowl of cornflakes,' wailed Poppy.

'There will be a canteen on site, I'm sure they will give us lunch,' her sister replied.

Once again they cycled along Ferry road and arrived at the fairground with minutes to spare.

'Hello there,' said the props girl as she came over to them.

'My name's Jane but usually I just get called "props". Mr. McLeod has asked me to look after you all. I'll show you around first shall I?'

She led the way through the fairground passing the cheeky boy on the dodgems. He was busy polishing the cars but waved to them and winked in Lily and Melanie's direction.

Indicating rows of caravans, Jane said,

'These belong to the fairground folk and are out of bounds to us but those over there are our dressing room vans, rest room and canteen.'

She opened the door to one caravan and said,

'This will be where you rest or get changed if need be.'

The children were surprised how spacious the van

was with luxurious seating, chrome rails to hang clothes and a sturdy table which was covered with magazines.

They all realised that there were times when you had to sit and wait to be called on set.

Outside Jane led them to another van; this looked rather like a hot dog stall with the side open from which two ladies were busy serving a group of actors and actresses with coffee.

The actress, Juliette Carlton, was sitting at a table with two men.

'Hi, you are the children for the chase scene, aren't you?' she asked in a friendly voice with no hint of yesterday's sulks.

'Yes Miss Carlton,' Toby replied. 'We are all excited and raring to go.'

She laughed and said,

'Let me introduce you to my leading man Adam Shaw and the villain of the plot Mark Blake.'

Mark Blake acknowledged the children with a smile and said,

'I hope you are all going to enjoy this experience but I'll warn you it can be very hard work.'

'We're not afraid of hard work,' put in Toby. 'I'm keen to learn all I can, 'I wouldn't mind being an actor when I'm older.'

'I'm sure you are all going to be "naturals". Don't you think so Adam?'

Adam Shaw muttered,

'Amateurs. Kids all over the set, getting in the way.' With that he got up and walked away.

'Take no notice, we're not all miserable like him,' Mark Blake told them.

'Come on, what would you all like to drink?' Jane asked them.

'We don't get a break until 11 a.m. so make the most of it now.'

They collected drinks from the canteen and sat talking to Mark Blake and Juliette Carlton.

Basil McLeod, the producer and director arrived on set and soon everyone was busy carrying out their various jobs before the days rehearsals could begin.

Firstly he approached the children and outlined the plot, giving them details of their parts. He produced scripts showing the lines they would have to remember. There weren't that many, it would be easy to learn them before they had to start filming their scene.

'We only rehearse today and tomorrow morning. We will actually start filming your scene the day after tomorrow and then not until the evening when the fair is open and in full swing,' Basil McLeod explained.

At 11 a.m. the crew and cast stopped for coffee break.

'Goodness I'm ready for a rest,' said Lily 'I didn't realise how tiring it would be. I don't like working with Adam Shaw, he isn't very friendly or helpful is he?'

'I like the baddy though,' said Poppy and everyone laughed.

'Yes I must admit Mark is very nice for a baddy and very good looking,' agreed Melanie.

The rest of the morning and afternoon were spent with more rehearsals, camera shot tests and even a visit to the make-up artist to arrange suitable make up for the children.

The makeup artist applied test colours to each of

the children's faces and when a suitable tint had been found she recorded this against their name.

Toby had made a fuss about being made up, saying it was sissy. He was soon won over when the make-up artist told him stories concerning some of the actors who had to have extensive make up to make them look the part when appearing in horror films.

Back on the set rehearsals continued, the children were put through their paces again and again. When they all thought Poppy looked as if she would drop from fatigue Basis McLeod shouted,

'Right, let's call it a day. I'll see everyone on set, 9 a.m. sharp.'

Turning to the children he said,

'Well done everyone, you are natural actors. Tomorrow we will go through your scene again but you should be finished by noon. You can have lunch and then you can have the rest of the day to yourselves. 9 a.m. don't forget.'

With that parting remark he strode away to his caravan.

'Do you realise what that means?' Toby asked.

'We can join the crabbing competition tomorrow. If we eat our lunch quickly and then set off, we could be back to Walberswick by 2 o'clock in time to enter. We had better go and buy some lines and bait this afternoon. You girls are entering the competition aren't you?'

'Of course we are,' retorted Melanie. Lily and Poppy eagerly agreed but Sarah wasn't so sure. Reluctantly she nodded; she certainly wasn't going to be left out.

They set off on their bikes back into the town to find a wet fish shop to supply them with bait.

'*Poo* it pongs a bit,' said Poppy wrinkling her nose.

'*Disgusting,*' put in Sarah, also pulling a face.

Toby, Melanie and Lily laughed at the comical faces Sarah and Poppy were pulling.

By the time they had found a shop to buy crabbing lines they were beginning to feel weary. They made their purchases then Toby said,

'Bakers next, I'll get a French stick to go with the cheese and fruit for tea.'

By the time they got back to the caravan even Toby felt exhausted.

'I would never have thought that acting was harder work than playing a game of football on a muddy pitch,' he declared as they sat around the table eating their meal.

'At least we haven't got much to wash up,' Melanie said as she cleared the plates away after the meal.

'I suggest we have an early night,' said Lily. 'Look at Poppy, she's asleep already.'

'Good idea,' said Toby. He picked up Poppy and carried her to her bunk.

'Night everyone, early start tomorrow,' Toby said as he closed the door behind him.

4

Crabbing and Old Friends

The children all managed to wake on time the next morning, even Poppy. They had a quick breakfast, washed the dishes and still managed to arrive on set by 9.a.m.

It was exciting to rehearse the "chase" scene which included their own small parts. Even the cheeky dodgems car boy had a small part much to Lily's and Melanie's amusement. There were one or two technical hitches with the "rides" which took a while to sort out, and lots of standing around but Toby said he didn't mind that as it gave him the chance to watch real actors on the job. The children continued to work hard all morning and the time passed very quickly.

'Lunch time already,' queried Poppy in surprise when Basil McLeod called,

'OK, lunch everybody.'

'I don't think I can face any lunch,' said Melanie, looking a bit green around the gills.

'Having to rehearse that scene on the wiz cars several times has left me feeling quite sick.'

'We need to have lunch quickly then we can set off to enter the crabbing competition,' Toby reminded them.

Sarah had been enjoying the rehearsing so much that

had forgotten all about the horrid crabbing competition.

All but Melanie; ate a hearty lunch after which they called goodbye to the cast and crew.

'See you tomorrow afternoon,' called out Juliette Carlton as the children left.

'Quickly, it's nearly two o'clock and we still have to collect the bait and lines from the caravan,' said Toby.

They locked their bikes together outside the caravan and collected the lines and the bait was put in a bucket. Quickly they made their way to the Bailey bridge as Walberswick was on the other side of the river.

There was already a large group patiently waiting to start when the five arrived puffing and panting. They just made it in time.

An official looking man holding a clip-board was taking entries, they joined the queue to give their names and ages.

Groups of friends went off to find their own favourite positions along a stream that ran out to sea.

'Follow me,' said Toby. 'I've been here before and know a good spot.' He led them over the wooden bridge to the other side of the stream.

There were already four children in the spot he had picked and the eldest boy looked up at their approach.

'Toby Richards! The boy exclaimed. 'What a surprise, have you come up from Leiston just for the crabbing competition?'

'Hello Ollie, what a coincidence, fancy seeing you here.' Toby smiled at Ollie's brother and young twin sisters. They just smiled back shyly.

'I haven't seen you since you moved to Halesworth and no we aren't just here for the competition but I'll tell you why, once we get under way.'

Toby introduced Ollie to the girls then said,

'We won't have much chance of winning the crabbing competition if Ollie has entered, he is a very keen fisherman and very lucky.'

'Oh, I don't know, I think us girls could win if we put our minds to it,' replied Lily.

They all settled down on the bank, unravelled their lines and hooked on the smelly bait. Toby had to put Sarah's bait on her line as she wouldn't touch it herself.

The official looking man picked up a megaphone and proceeded to get everybody, including the parents, to be quiet. He gave details of the rules then looked at his watch and at two-thirty he shouted, 'Ready *GO*'.

There was much excitement as children of all ages lowered their lines into the water.

Toby and Ollie had time to catch up on each other's news as they cast their lines repeatedly. It was fun, feeling the tug of a crab on the line, but trying to bring the line up to the net without the crab falling back into the water was an art in itself.

'Oh I've just lost a big one,' wailed Sarah getting carried away with all the excitement around her and forgetting she was scared of creepy things.

'I've got three small ones,' said Poppy, looking into the plastic bucket.

'You'll need to do better than that,' Ollie said as he threw a small crab he had just caught back into the water.

The weather was perfect for the afternoon. Clear blue sky, not too hot with a cool breeze coming off the sea.

The ice-cream van was doing a roaring trade with

Mums and Dads being sent off to buy various ice delights as their respective children were all intent on checking their lines. The atmosphere of the afternoon was often intense as everyone tried their hardest to catch a particularly large crab. Squeals of disappointment could be heard as crabs were lost back to the murky water time after time.

The official blew a whistle when the time was up. Everyone began to wind up their line ready for the weigh in.

'My line's all caught up with yours,' Sarah told Poppy. They tried to unravel them but had to get Toby to help them in the end.

'Still we both have a good-sized crab each haven't we?' Poppy said to Sarah.

'I know, but have you seen the size of Ollie's crab? It's huge, it must be a winner.'

She was right, Ollie's was the winning crab, every one clapped as he went up to collect his prize.

His parents had returned in time to see the weigh in and Ollie's father said,

'This deserves a celebration, what do you children think?' he said looking at them all.

'I know, why don't we have a picnic in the sand dunes?' suggested Poppy.

'That sounds a lovely idea,' Ollie's mother said. 'I'll pop to the local shop to buy some nice things for tea, we don't want to eat up all your rations,' she continued laughing.

Whilst Ollie's mum drove to the shops, the others walked back to the caravan and all helped to gather up plates and cutlery for the picnic.

Ollie's mum soon returned with a couple of bags containing, rolls, ham, cheese, cakes and even tubs of jelly. Everything was placed in carrier bags. To lighten the load everyone had to carry a bag to the beach.

The twins, Sarah and Poppy played at the water's edge whilst the older children spread out plates of food on a tartan rug.

After the meal, they played cricket on the flat dunes and as the sun began to go down Toby, Ollie and Johnny decided to make a camp fire. They found some large stones which they used to circle a shallow hole in the sand, then collected the dry driftwood and soon had a fire going.

Ollie's dad started singing songs which he remembered from his scouting days and everyone was able to join in with the more familiar ones.

The fire began to die down. Poppy and the twins were having a job to keep their eyes open.

'Time to go home,' said Ollie's dad.

He bent down to pick up one of the twins who had fallen asleep. Ollie helped his mother with his other sister whilst Johnny was left to carry their belongings.

'It's been great seeing you again and meeting your friends. I'll cycle over to see you all soon if you don't mind having me around,' Ollie said to Toby.

'Come whenever you like,' replied Toby, the girls eagerly agreeing with him. They had all liked Toby's friend.

'Night,' they all called as Ollie and his family drove away.

None of them little realised, how glad they were going to be when they next saw Ollie.

5

Assignation

It was 8 a.m. before anyone woke the following morning.

Toby opened the caravan door and called out cheerfully,

'Come on, don't let's waste the morning sleeping, how about we walk along the beach to the pier? We can work up an appetite for lunch which we can get on the film set before we start afternoon rehearsals.'

Lily yawned, stretched her arms and replied,

'OK, that's a good idea.'

Toby left to go and get dressed in the shower block.

'Poppy and I have never been on the pier. Have you Sarah?' Lily asked.

'Oh yes, it's great fun, although I'm not too keen on seeing the sea between the gaps in the planks beneath my feet.'

'I like watching the clock near the end of the pier. It pours water on a metal man in the bath on the half hour,' put in Melanie.

The girls dressed, and then laid the table for breakfast. They gobbled down their cornflakes, swigged back the orange juice and had finished by the time Toby returned.

It didn't take him too long to catch up, with Melanie

whipping his bowl from under his nose as soon as he had finished.

They walked through the sand dunes, watching children flying kites as they went.

Once upon the promenade it was an easy walk to the pier. It was very busy, holidaymakers jostled each other as they looked around the amusements and at the far end of the pier fishermen were busy casting their lines into the sea.

As they drew nearer to them, Poppy said softly,

'Look isn't that Adam Shaw from the film set?'

Juliette Carlton's leading man was in earnest conversation with a rough looking man.

'I wonder how he knows him; it doesn't look as if they are just passing the time of day together. The conversation seems very intense,' said Lily.

Adam Shaw left the fisherman and walked briskly in their direction. They all turned to look over the side of the pier so that he wouldn't notice them.

'Hey, that man's the fisherman who didn't like us looking at his boat. I didn't recognise him at first,' said Melanie.

'You're right,' said Toby. 'I wonder what those two have in common. I don't think Adam Shaw is arranging to buy fish, do you?'

'No, but something smells fishy to me,' said Poppy.

'He must be going back to the film set now. It's time we made our way there too, so let's keep him in our sights,' said Toby.

They all thought that this was a good idea and followed the path Adam Shaw had taken but at a more leisurely pace.

'I'm rather nervous about tonight's filming even though I'm looking forward to being in a film,' said Lily.

'I just hope we don't have to rehearse that 'wiz car' ride more than once or the make-up girl will have her work cut out trying to disguise my green face,' Melanie said dolefully. The children's steps got quicker the more they talked about the coming filming and the more excited they all became.

In no time at all they had reached the fun fair. They waved and called hello to the dodgem boy as they walked over to the canteen. Most of the actors were drinking coffee waiting patiently for Mr. McLeod to appear.

Adam Shaw was nowhere to be seen.

'Hello,' Juliette Carlton said, smiling as the children approached the canteen van. 'Come and have lunch. You must try these sticky buns, they are really nice.'

This was said in between Juliette delicately licking her fingers. 'These jam doughnuts are delicious, I can thoroughly recommend them.'

The children laughed and queued at the hatchway for a salad lunch. They all took Juliette's advice and helped themselves to a sticky doughnut each.

'Can we sit with you Miss Carlton?' Poppy asked.

'Of course you can, there is plenty of room for all of you. I wonder where Mark and Adam have got to?' she said, looking about the set.

'We followed Mr. Shaw up from the pier, he was just in front of us so he must be here somewhere,' said Lily.

'They don't want to be late or Basil will be in a foul mood for the whole day. I can assure you that would be a most unpleasant experience for you all.'

Juliette Carlton had just finished speaking when Basil

McLeod came out of his caravan at the same time as Mark Blake and Adam Shaw arrived on set.

Mark went over to Juliette and began to speak to her as Basil McLeod called out, 'Quiet everyone, let's get this show on the road.'

The cast and crew all began to take up their various positions. Toby overheard some of Juliette and Mark's conversation.

'He was acting most peculiarly, he looked around but didn't see me and then he tried the door of your caravan,' he whispered to her.

Toby didn't hear anymore as Mr. McLeod was shouting orders through the megaphone again and getting very irate. Everyone was kept very busy rehearsing their parts for the rest of the afternoon.

At 4.30 Basil McLeod called a halt for dinner.

'Back on set at 5.30 for makeup and lighting checks everyone,' he called as he strode off towards his van.

'I'm famished,' groaned Sarah.

'Let's get to the canteen before a queue forms,' said Melanie setting off towards the van, she was quickly followed by the others.

They collected their dinners on trays and found a table.

'Quickly before Miss Carlton comes over and joins us. I want to tell you what I heard earlier.'

They sat down and bent forward listening to Toby as he recounted the conversation he had overheard.

'I wonder who was trying her caravan door,' Lily queried.

'I bet it was that horrid Adam Shaw, I think he could be capable of anything,' said Melanie.

'Perhaps he was trying to steal Miss Carlton's diamond pendant,' suggested Poppy innocently.

'We can't say that, we haven't any evidence to suggest he would, have we?' Toby said seriously.

'He's a baddie and I think we should keep an eye on him,' Poppy retorted.

They all agreed it would be a good idea to be vigilant and watch Adam Shaw's movements in case he was up to no good.

Basil McLeod called everyone to order again using the megaphone.

Time for the cameras to roll!

Suddenly the children felt very apprehensive. This was *IT*, their big moment. They were only on the screen for a short while but their friends would still be able to recognise them and be impressed when the film was released. Their clothing had already been checked for suitability for the filming but where necessary, replacements were quickly supplied.

The make-up girl applied the correct colouring to their faces so that the artificial lights didn't give them a green or orange looking skin.

'I'm sure I'll still look green after that wiz ride,' wailed Melanie as the girl applied a tint to her face, followed by face powder.

'Don't you worry young lady, you will look just fine,' said the makeup girl shooing Melanie and the others out of her van with a laugh.

The fairground was in full swing, the colourful lights were shining around the numerous stalls and rides.

The smell of hot dogs and onions filled the air, together with the sweeter smell of burnt sugar from the candy floss machine.

The crowd was bigger than usual as it was known that filming was taking place that night and many locals hoped to be in the crowd scenes.

Mr. McLeod took them all through the chase scene first and as the sky darkened the crew prepared the lightning ready for filming to begin.

Toby looking around in wonder said,

'This is the life for me; I definitely want to be an actor when I get older.'

'I wouldn't mind being an actress myself,' said Lily.

'What about you Sarah, do you fancy being an actress?' asked Poppy.

'No fear, it's much too much like hard work and I like my meals at a regular time.'

'Look isn't that the fisherman that Adam Shaw was talking to on the pier this morning?' Poppy said pointing to a man standing by the Hoop-la stall.

They all followed her gaze towards the stall, and sure enough the fisherman stood there. He was throwing the hoops but in a disinterested way and he kept looking about furtively as if he were waiting for something to happen at any moment.

'How odd; I wouldn't have thought a fairground was his idea of entertainment, he looks so out of place here,' said Lily.

'I suggest we keep our eyes on him,' said Toby.

Just then the children were called over to begin filming the chase scene.

It was so exciting they forgot about being nervous but more importantly they forgot to keep an eye on the fisherman.

The scene involved Miss Carlton being used as a hostage by Mark Blake while her film husband Adam Shaw tried to rescue her, chasing after the two of them through the fairground. The children's small parts entailed helping to trip the bad guy up so she could escape his clutches.

The scene ended in a brawl with the two men fighting near the Hoop-la stall. Whilst this part was being filmed no one noticed a fisherman stoop down and pick something up from under the stall. All eyes were on the actors fighting, including the children's.

The scene concluded with the police arriving and wrestling the bad guy away from the hero and carting the villain off to jail.

'*CUT,*' shouted Basil McLeod.

'That was a take,' he said. 'Well done everyone, it went like clockwork for a change.'

He turned to the children and said,

'You all did a great job. Did you enjoy it?'

'Oh yes,' they all chorused.

'It was *brilliant*,' put in an excited and wide-eyed Poppy.

'We still have more to film yet. Your parts are finished but you are more than welcome to come and watch the rest of the filming if you wish,' Basil McLeod told them.

'Tomorrow is our last day and we finish with a bit of a celebration in the evening, please come along and join the party.'

The children said they would and then called goodnight to the rest of the cast and crew and wearily went to get into the car Mr. McLeod had laid on to take them back to the caravan.

'Well, what an exciting evening,' said Melanie when they arrived back.

'Yes, it will be nice to have a really relaxing day tomorrow! Toby said.

6

A Quiet Early Morning Walk!

'Hello, anyone about?'

'Oh hello Miss Wells, said Toby poking his head from under the caravan. 'This is an early visit, isn't it?' he replied rubbing his eyes.

'Not really, it is 11 a.m. you know,' she replied smiling.

'Goodness, we were going to go and watch the rest of the filming this morning,' he replied.

'I know, I went to the film set first, the props girl said they were expecting you all this morning. She did add that you all looked extremely tired last night and that it had been quite late when you had left the set.'

This conversation awoke the other children. Miss Wells entered the caravan and said, 'Shall I join you all for brunch?'

'What's brunch?' Poppy asked.

'Idiot, it's too late for breakfast and too early for lunch, so we have brunch instead,' said Lily to her sister.

'I like the sound of that,' said Sarah.

'I've come prepared with a few extra rations,' laughed Miss Wells.

The meal turned out to be a bit unusual.

They started with cornflakes, then had boiled eggs with toasted fingers or soldiers as Poppy called them. This was followed by some lovely warm croissants and apricot jam.

'I like brunch,' declared Poppy.

'I think we ought to have it every day,' said Sarah.

The others laughed but agreed with her.

'Now what are you all going to do today?' Miss Wells asked them.

'Not much, just laze about I expect,' Melanie informed her.

'I'm going back to have lunch with Basil McLeod but I'll be back in time for the party this evening though. You will all be there, won't you?' she asked them.

'There's no way we are going to miss that,' Toby said.

'Please apologise for us for not going to watch filming this morning.'

'OK, I'll do that, but don't worry I expect everyone will realise you all overslept. I'll see you all tonight then,' Miss Wells said getting to her feet.

'I'll leave the dishes for you to do,' she said, waving as she walked off towards her car.

'Come on,' said Toby, 'Let's clear away quickly and go out for a walk down by the harbour.'

It didn't take them long when they all mucked in to help without arguing or fighting.

Soon they were on their way walking this time along the pot holed road beside the river. They stopped and bought ice creams from the Chandlery, they watched a fisherman mending his nets.

'I wonder if Ollie will come over to see us today,' Sarah asked.

'I hope so,' said Poppy. 'We had a good time with Ollie and his family.'

'It's a long way for him to cycle though,' put in Melanie.

'If Ollie says he will cycle over to see us, he will,' replied Toby.

'Well I hope so too, I liked him,' said Lily.

Sarah suddenly let out a yell.

'*LOOK*, on the far side of the river, it's that fisherman friend of Adam Shaw. We forgot all about watching him last night. It looks as if he is getting ready to set sail.'

True enough, the fisherman was obviously getting ready to set sail, making all the necessary checks, prior to casting off.

'I thought fishermen went out to sea very early in the morning,' said Melanie.

'They do usually, I wonder where he is going at this time of day,' Toby queried.

'Let's sit here and watch him,' suggested Poppy as she busily tried to lick the ice cream that was melting and running down the side of the cornet.

The fisherman made several trips back and forwards from his hut to the boat carrying equipment and packages.

'It looks as if he is clearing off for good,' said Lily.

The fisherman shut his hut and strode off towards the village of Walberswick.

'Quick, let's see if we can find out what he has been packing away,' said Toby.

'We've got a good walk down to and over the Bailey bridge and up the other side of the river to his hut,' said Melanie. 'He might come back before we get there.'

'Not if we run,' said Lily who was already following Toby.

'Come on then girls,' said Melanie grabbing Poppy and Sarah's hands.

It was hard going, especially on the other side of the river where the footpath was very eroded in places.

Toby was keeping an eye open for the fisherman.

'I expect he's gone to the pub for his lunch before he sets off,' he said.

A bit muddy from the occasional slip and all out of breath, they finally reached the hut. Toby looked around cautiously to see if anyone was watching but Melanie opened the door and marched brazenly into the hut.

'Melanie,' Lily called after her. 'Say he comes back.'

Melanie popped her head around the door and said,

'Come on, let's look quickly then.'

'Poppy, can you stay outside and keep guard, if you see him coming back, give a knock on the door,' said Toby.

Poppy agreed to stand guard and the others followed Lily into the hut.

The inside of the hut was dark and smelt of tar and fish. There was one small grimy window high on the back wall. This didn't let in much light as it had a security grill covering it. When the children's eyes were accustomed to the dark interior they saw that it was practically empty. A large holdall stood on a bench behind the door out of sight of anyone just looking into the hut. The floor was dusty and showed clean patches where items had been removed from the room.

Toby moved over to the holdall and unzipped it. He rummaged around in the clothes and withdrew an oblong black leather covered box.

The children crowded around as he opened the box to expose Juliette Carlton's beautiful diamond pendant lying on a cushion of black velvet.

'*WOW!*' said Melanie and Lily at the same time.

'How did the fisherman get hold of it?' Sarah asked.

'He stole it of course,' replied Toby.

'But how?' was Lily's next question.

'I bet I know,' Toby said. 'You know Mark said he had seen someone at Juliette's caravan door, well I reckon Adam Shaw stole it when he had the opportunity and passed it to the fisherman when we were filming in the evening.'

'Yes, remember we saw the fisherman by the Hoop-la stall,' said Sarah.

'With all the confusion as the fight scene was filmed,' put in Melanie, 'he could easily have slipped it to the fisherman.'

Lily was busy taking the pendant out of its box and thinking she would try it on when a great commotion was heard outside.

Poppy gave out a wail and then the door was pushed open with such a force and there stood the fisherman gripping poor Poppy with one hand and the other was over her mouth. There was a look of thunder about his face.

'*Let her go you BRUTE,*' shouted Toby.

'*What do you kids think you are doing in MY hut?*' he roared. 'Stealing my things, I reckon. I'll have the police on you.'

'Really,' said Toby in a sarcastic voice. 'Are you going to show them your new diamond necklace?'

The fisherman looked down at the closed box in Lily's hand. He shoved Poppy across the room against Toby which made him fall over.

The fisherman grabbed up his holdall and snatched the box from Lily's hand, shoved it into the holdall and pushed her towards the others and then quickly opened the door and shut it behind him.

In the confusion, Poppy started crying, Melanie helped her up off the floor, Toby jumped up with a helping hand from Lily.

The sound of a bar being dropped into place and a key being turned in the lock was heard.

Sarah rushed to the door but as hard as she tried she could not budge it. She started to cry. Toby had a go but no matter what he did it wouldn't budge.

'He's well and truly locked us in,' said Toby in disbelief.

'We can't get out of the window, we shall have to shout altogether, hoping we are heard by passers-by,' said Melanie.

7

Ollie to the Rescue

The five children all started to shout at the tops of their voices, or rather four of them did but Sarah continued to sob bitterly.

'Don't cry,' said Toby, 'we will soon get out of here, there are plenty of holiday makers about and the ferryman is bound to hear us when he reaches this side of the river.'

The only problem was, the ferryman had stopped on the other side to go off for his lunch. Similarly the quay-side was deserted as the holiday-makers had also wandered off to find somewhere to have their own lunches.

After banging and shouting for what seemed ages, the children gave up and sat on the bench.

'Well, what happens now?' Melanie said with a sigh.

Unbeknown to them there had been a witness to their going into the hut. Ollie was cycling down the harbour road on the Southwold side of the river and had seen the fisherman lock the children into the hut; he couldn't for the life of him understand why the man should do that. He cycled as fast as he could, dodging pot holes, past the Chandlery and boat clubhouse, over the Bailey bridge he clanged on his bike, he then had a very rough ride along the muddy footpath on the Walberswick side of the river.

When at last he came to the row of fishermen's huts he was out of breath. The fisherman's boat had left her mooring and Ollie watched it heading out to sea.

Now which hut was it he wondered, they all looked alike. He laid his bike down and listened. Was that someone sobbing? He walked along the row of huts and stopped outside the one where the sobbing sounded.

'Hello there,' he called. 'It's me, Ollie, are you all OK?'

The five children all started shouting out at once.

'Yes, we've been locked in, can you get us out?' Toby asked amidst the din.

'The keys been taken away, I'll have to try to break the lock. I've got some spanners and screwdrivers in my bicycle kit, I'll get them.'

He fetched the kit and quickly began to try to prise the lock open. He looked around the ground and found a large rock to use as a hammer. In the hut the others waited impatiently, calling out to ask how he was getting on every few seconds.

Finally the lock gave way, Ollie raised the bar and five bedraggled looking children stumbled through the doorway, blinking in the bright sunshine.

What a sorry sight they looked, Sarah had red swollen eyes, their clothes were covered in dust and they all looked very dishevelled.

They all tried talking at once but at last Ollie managed to get Toby to explain how come they were all locked in the hut by the fisherman.

'He has got away with Juliette Carlton's beautiful

diamond pendant,' said Poppy.

'Oh no he hasn't,' said Lily pulling down the collar of her tee shirt to reveal the fabulous giant diamond, glittering in the afternoon sun.

'Lily you are clever,' squealed Poppy, cheering up considerably.

Ollie looked at the diamond in amazement and said,

'Gosh, it must be worth a fortune, does Miss Carlton know it has been stolen?'

'I don't know. I wonder if she noticed it was missing this morning, we had better get back to the fairground,' said Toby.

'Here's the ferryman again, let's cross by boat it will be quicker,' said Melanie.

'Oh, that's a good idea Melanie, I don't think I've got enough energy to walk anyway,' said poor Sarah.

'You had better hide that necklace under your top,' said Toby as Lily and Melanie were still admiring it with envy.

They helped Ollie to get his bike on board and had just enough room left for them to squeeze onto the small boat. It was a good job that no one else was waiting to cross.

The ferryman rowed, with powerful, confident strokes and they were soon on the Southwold side of the river.

What a quiet day indeed, thought Lily to herself as they collected their bikes from the caravan to cycle with Ollie to the fairground.

8

What a Commotion

The six children pushed their bikes into the fairground to find a commotion going on.

The place seemed to be swarming with policemen who were obviously going from caravan to caravan questioning the occupants.

'It looks as if the theft has been discovered afterall,' said Toby.

Juliette Carlton seemed to be the centre of the commotion. Her voice, carrying clearly across the fairground.

'Officer, I've told you already I put the pendant in my locked jewellery case when Mr. McLeod said I couldn't wear it on set. I didn't find it was missing until I went to put it on after this morning's shoot. I hadn't even noticed that the jewel box had been forced open. As soon as we finished last night I went back to my van and was asleep almost as soon as my head hit the pillow. This morning I overslept, so I dressed quickly and dashed out to the makeup van, not even looking at my own dressing table,' Juliette Carlton told the police officer in an angry voice.

'Don't worry Miss Carlton, my men are searching now, we may even find it on site,' the officer said in an unconvincing voice.

The children walked over towards the group and were surprised to see Miss Wells seated at a table with Basil McLeod, an unfinished meal in front of them.

An emotional Juliette Carlton was pacing up and down and Mark Blake was trying desperately to console her.

'I'll never see my lovely diamond pendant again, it will be miles away from here by now,' she wailed looking at the Detective Chief Inspector who was still taking notes from the other actors standing nearby.

Lily had quietly taken the necklace from around her neck, holding it tightly in her hand she stepped forward.

'Oh yes you will,' it isn't miles away, it's right here,' she said holding her hand out.

Juliette Carlton rushed forward exclaiming in astonishment,

'Where on earth did you find it?'

She fastened it around her own neck, a rapturous smile upon her face.

Adam Shaw had just joined the group by the canteen van. Lily saw an expression of utter amazement come over his face. She nudged Toby and whispered to the others, 'Look at Adam Shaw's face, he certainly didn't expect to see that pendant here.'

The police officer went up to Lily and said in a stern voice,

'Now miss I think we had better hear how you came to be in possession of Miss Carlton's necklace.'

Miss Wells got up from her seat and said,

'Officer these children are my pupils and I can vouch for their honesty. I'm sure there is a perfectly plausible reason for Lily to have the pendant in her possession.'

'Oh Miss Wells, we have had an adventure, just wait until you hear our story,' gasped Poppy.

'We were locked up by a fisherman in his hut; he was making a run for it by boat. Ollie came and rescued us,' put in Toby.

'Well I never,' Miss Wells replied.

The D.C.I turned to Toby and said,

'You seem to be the oldest. Now can you start at the beginning and give me a clear account of what's been going on?'

'Yes sir,' Toby replied, and he then proceeded to recount the day's events to the policeman.

9

The Chase is On

Adam Shaw was edging slowly away from the crowd of film crew and fairground folk who had gathered to hear what was being said. He was trying to make his way towards his caravan.

Toby looked him straight in the eye and then turned and said to the DCI, 'We think the pendant was stolen by someone on the film set.'

A gasp of astonishment went up from the crowd of film people.

'We think the fisherman was only the accomplice and he was obviously going off to dispose of the jewel on the thief's behalf,' Toby explained.

He was still keeping his eye on Adam Shaw and as Toby finished speaking the actor made a sudden dash across the fairground.

'Quick he is trying to escape,' shouted Ollie, legging if after Adam Shaw followed by Toby, Melanie and Lily.

'Oh, no you don't,' said Miss Wells, as Sarah and Poppy started to follow them.

'I don't know what your parents are going to say to all this. I'm certainly not letting you two out of my sight.'

The DCI looked flustered as he watched the older children give chase.

'We think the thief is Mr. Shaw,' gabbled Poppy, struggling to get out of Miss Wells' grip.

'He looked pretty amazed when he saw that my sister had the pendant.'

The DCI shouted to his men,

'Apprehend that man.'

Whistles blew and pandemonium broke loose.

Mark Blake gave chase as Juliette Carlton sank into a chair next to Basil McLeod.

He was speechless for once. Miss Wells stared at the diamond pendant around Juliette Carlton's neck. So pretty a thing to cause all this bother.

The fairground had been in full swing for some time and was filling up fast with holidaymakers.

Adam Shaw was dodging in and around side shows trying to lose the policemen giving chase. He jumped onto the carousel which was just beginning to gather speed.

Toby and Ollie managed to get on board, as did a burley policeman.

The people on the ride looked on in amazement as the constable grabbed the actor and wrestled with him under the wooden horses which were going up and down over their bodies.

Toby managed to fling himself against Adam Shaw, knocking him back down as he tried to get away from the constable. In doing so he fell against Ollie who stumbled and fell against the lever which regulated the rides speed. The carousel began to go faster and faster. The wooden horses galloped up and down so fast Adam Shaw and the constable hadn't a chance of getting to their feet.

'HEY!' shouted the man collecting the fares. 'Push that lever back, we are going much too fast.'

The passengers started to scream as the carousel went faster and faster. Mark Blake, Lily and Melanie watched in horror.

'Oh, be careful Toby,' shouted Melanie as Toby nearly fell off of the ride only to be pulled back by Ollie's quick action in grabbing his shirt.

The man in charge of the ride, who was use to walking about on it, managed to reach the lever and push it back to the correct position.

As it slowed down Adam Shaw tried to get away but being very giddy he just fell off of the carousel into the arms of three waiting policemen.

'Take him away,' said the DCI coming up to them. 'I'll question him at the station.'

He turned to the children and said,

'Let's return to your teacher, I'll need a full description of the fisherman. Did you get the name of his boat by the way?'

'I did,' said Toby. 'I noticed it that first day when he grabbed hold of me and told us all to clear off. It's called *An ill wind* and I thought what an odd name.'

The DCI laughed,

'Well, it's going to be an ill wind for him when we catch him, which we will, especially as I expect you can give us a very good description of him,' he said to Toby.

They had re-joined the others by now and everyone started laughing except Sarah.

'What's funny about that?' she said.

'An ill wind blows no good' so the saying goes,' Miss Wells explained.

'I really thought I had lost my pendant for good,' said Juliette Carlton.

'Well perhaps you will now take my advice,' put in Basil McLeod. 'Have it locked in a proper safe, wear it only for special occasions,' he continued.

'Darling you are so right,' purred Juliette, her eyes sparkling. 'I'll wear it tonight at our celebration party.'

Basil McLeod groaned, got up and walked away saying,

'Women, I give up.'

10

It's a Wrap

'Do you realise,' said Poppy, 'it's 5.30 and we haven't had anything to eat since brunch? I thought I was feeling a bit peculiar.'

'Huh,' snorted Lily, 'You are always peculiar.'

'She's right though,' said Melanie. 'We have missed a meal. What about you, Ollie, aren't you hungry?'

'You bet, I haven't had anything to eat since breakfast and that was very early this morning.'

Juliette Carlton had retired to her caravan to rest before the evening's party.

Miss Wells and the children were sitting watching the film crew pack up as this conversation about food took place.

'Well in all the excitement I didn't get to finish my meal with Mr. McLeod so how about I treat you all to fish and chips?' Miss Wells asked them.

This invitation was greeted with great enthusiasm by all.

'I just want to have a quick word with Mr. McLeod before we go. I'll only be a minute,' she said.

As good as her word she returned after a short absence.

'Mr. McLeod has agreed to my inviting all of Ollie's

family to the party tonight. What do you think, will they come, Ollie?'

'Oh great, thanks, yes I'm sure they would love to come,' Ollie replied.

'I know everyone else's parents are coming, I feel I must apologise to them all. If I hadn't suggested these film parts you wouldn't have been involved in this adventure. Let's go to the fish shop and while we queue I'll phone your parents Ollie.

It didn't take too long to reach the fish and chip shop. The queue was fairly short and soon they were all sitting on a bench overlooking the sea enjoying their meal.

'Perhaps we might hear from the police later as to whether they have been able to trace the fisherman,' said Toby between mouthfuls of chips.

'They have a coastguard here at Southwold,' Ollie told them.

'I expect he was alerted, they should soon pick the fisherman up, it's only a matter of time.'

Ollie's mother had agreed they would all come to the party and had received the brief details of the day's happenings with surprise. Miss Wells had also informed the other parents, but told them they would hear the full story at the party that night.

'I'm going home to change. I suggest you take Ollie back to the caravan with you, have a good clean up, then a rest. See you all this evening.'

With that she walked back to the fairground to collect her car and the children began their long walk back to the caravan.

They rested for half an hour then had a quick swim

in the sea to freshen up. They rummaged through their rucksacks to try to find the least dirty shorts and t-shirts to put on. Luckily Ollie's clothes weren't in such a state as the rest of them. They improved their appearances by giving their hair a good brush and were soon ready to return to the fairground.

The film set site had undergone a drastic transformation. The lighting had been left to illuminate the party area but all the other equipment had been packed away. Tables and chairs had been set out and a long trestle table was laden with party type food.

'*Wow,*' said Poppy, eyeing the food greedily.

'What a spread, the catering staff have put on,' said Melanie.

'Look,' said Lily they are even setting up a disco, great.'

Sure enough a small area had been cleared for dancing and a local band were busy setting up their equipment.

Toby wandered over to look at the bands gear. Besides having visions of being an actor he also fancied the idea of being a pop DJ.

'It looks as if we are going to have a fun night,' said Miss Wells, approaching with Lily and Poppy's parents.

'Let's find ourselves a large table,' she said as Toby's, Melanie's and Sarah's parents arrived at the same time.

She turned to Ollie. 'Is that your family over there?' she said pointing to a couple with three children.

'Hi Mum, Dad over here,' Ollie yelled out.

Things got a bit noisy as Miss Wells tried to introduce everyone. The parents all wanted to know what had actually happened during the day.

As the story unfolded they were joined at the table by Juliette Carlton who insisted everyone called her Juliette and by Mr. McLeod and Mark Blake.

Juliette praised the children and thanked them yet again for finding her necklace which was duly admired by all the mums.

The party was in full swing when the police put in an appearance.

The DCI came over to their table and was introduced to the other grown-ups.

'You will be pleased to hear we have caught the fisherman, he was picked up landing at Felixstowe. We have had a statement from Mr. Shaw and it seems that he was approached by a man acting for a private collector who badly wanted to acquire your diamond Miss Carlton.

Mr. Shaw had run up a lot of gambling debts and he saw the opportunity of making some quick money if he stole your pendant for the collector.

We haven't yet found out how he got to know the fisherman but we do know that the fisherman's job was to deliver the jewel to the collector's contact.'

'Have you found out the name of the contact yet?' asked Sarah's dad.

'No sir, but I dare say a lot more information will be forthcoming when we continue to question them both,' the DCI explained.

'Now I'll leave you all to enjoy the rest of the evening and the rest of your holiday,' he said looking at the children with a smile on his face.

'Thank you once again for all your efforts in helping to thwart this crime.'

With that, he smiled, said goodbye and walked away.

'He is right of course, we can now get on and enjoy the rest of our holiday and not have any more adventures,' said Lily.

'Well not until the next holiday we have together,' piped up Poppy seriously.

Everyone laughed.

We shall just have to wait to see if Poppy's statement turns out to be correct, won't we?

Adventure at Winchelsea Beach

1

Oh no, chickenpox

Lily pushed open the door into her sister's darkened bedroom none too quietly and pulled back the curtains. A beam of sunlight fell directly on young Poppy's face; she groaned, rubbed her eyes, turned over to face the wall and at the same time pulled the duvet up over her head.

Lily looked into the dressing table mirror and wailed,

'Just look at my face! How can I start the summer holidays when I look like this? You expect the odd teenage spot or two but not to have your whole face covered in horrid scabby spots all at once.'

'Oh, close the curtains and go away Lily, I feel awful, my eyes are sore, my head aches and I'm itching all over.'

Lily realised she was being selfish. It was only a few days ago that she had felt exactly the same as her sister. She tiptoed over to the bed, sat down and put her arm around Poppy.

'Sorry sis. I'll go and get you a nice cold drink of Mum's lemonade.'

The girl's mother and father were deep in conversation when Lily entered the kitchen.

'There you are,' her mother said as Lily walked over to the fridge and took out the jug of lemonade.

'Your father thinks I need a rest after waiting on you girls these past two weeks, so he suggested you both go and stay with Aunt Mary in Kent. What do you think, would you like a couple of weeks at her guest house?'

'Oh, that would be great, I wouldn't have to face my friends looking like this, the spots, should all be gone by the time we came home.'

'Well actually, Dad thought that as your friend's Melanie and Toby were recovering from chickenpox and Poppy's friend Sarah is at the same stage as she is, you might all go on holiday together, that's if all the parents agree.'

Lily thought about it for a minute, an idea coming into her head.

'That's a good idea Dad, all five of us have spots and we won't meet anyone we know in Kent so I don't really mind going. I was just wondering though, you remember Toby's friend Ollie that rescued us from the fisherman's hut in Southwold last year.* It might be nice to invite him so that Toby doesn't feel out of it amongst us four girls.'

'I thought Ollie every bit as sensible as Toby and the two of them should be able to keep you girls in order,' her mother replied.

Lily raised her eyebrows and said in a peeved voice, 'Melanie and I are sensible enough to look after the young ones as well as ourselves thank you, mother.'

Her father got up and reached for the telephone.

'I'll ring your aunt right now. The guest house will be full as it's the start of the school holidays but she did tell me she was in the process of converting some old railways carriages that stand in the garden. If they are nearly ready, perhaps she will be able to put you all up in them.'

Lily waited patiently listening to her father's end of the conversation. He told her Aunt Mary that he would let her know for sure how many children there would be. Lily felt a thrill of excitement run through her. She hoped her friend's parents would agree to them coming on this holiday.

Her father put the telephone down,

'That's all fixed up then, all we need to do now is contact your friend's parents and of course Ollie's. We can then arrange a day to set off.'

'Mind you, it will be a good week before Poppy and Sarah are well enough to travel,' said Lily's mother.

'I might as well telephone everyone now and get things started,' Lily's father said.

He was on the telephone for quite some time but happily all the parents thought it a good idea for the children to have a change of scenery to convalesce. Lily's father suggested that they all take their bikes by train. It would enable them to explore the countryside and also build their strength up.

Lily took a tray up to her sister at teatime, propped her pillows up for her and quietly told her the arrangements for going to Kent.

Poppy immediately perked up.

'Really, we are all going together. I'm glad Ollie will be coming, You know what that means don't you?' she asked Lily.

'No?'

'We are bound to have yet another adventure,' said Poppy in excitement.

* see Southwold Adventure

2

The holiday begins

A week later the girl's father was busy oiling their bikes and checking the brakes to make sure they were road worthy.

'*MUM,*' yelled Lily down the stairs.

'We can't take all these clothes you have laid out on the bed, don't forget we have to carry it in rucksacks on our bikes, we only need a couple of pairs of old shorts, T-shirts, a jumper or two, wet weather clothes and our swimsuits.'

After much hunting around for torches, missing socks and the puncture kit for the bikes they were ready.

'Now remember Lily,' said her father. 'You are in charge; take care of your sister.'

Turning to look at Poppy he said, 'I expect you to be on your best behaviour, I don't want you leading Sarah astray.'

'What *me* Dad?' Poppy said innocently.

Finally they were ready, wheeling their bikes down the drive, they turned, waved goodbye to their parents and set off down the quiet leafy lane towards Sarah's home.

Sarah was waiting impatiently with her parents at their garden gate.

'Isn't it exciting, I'm dying to sleep in a railway carriage, the guest house is practically on the beach isn't it? Are we meeting Toby and Melanie at the station?'

'Yes and yes, to the two last questions,' replied Lily laughing as Sarah ran out of breath.

'Take no notice of Lily. I know you and me are going to be sharing a small bunk bedroom, it's going to be great fun,' Poppy said to her best friend.

'Come on you two, we don't want to miss the train. I bet Toby and Melanie are already waiting for us at the station,' said Lily.

Leaving Sarah's parents waving at the gate they cycled off towards the station.

The sisters had first made friends with Toby, Melanie and Sarah when they had moved from London to the remote Suffolk countryside several years ago. Straight away they fell headlong into a mystery and last summer they had all met up with Toby's friend Ollie in Southwold and had another adventure.

Was Poppy going to be proved right again this summer!

'Oh good,' said Poppy as the station came into view. She already felt tired trying to keep up, her bike only had three gears.

Sarah didn't say anything but she also welcomed the sight of the station. Like Poppy, her shorter legs had a job to keep pace with Lily on her new five-geared bike.

'Look there's Toby and Melanie,' Poppy called out as they wheeled their bikes onto the platform. Poppy tried to wheel her bike with one hand and wave with the other. The bike slipped to the ground stopping Lily in her tracks.

'For goodness sake Poppy, watch what you are doing, you nearly had the skin off my shins,' Lily said in a raised voice.

Toby came towards them smiling,

'Now girls, don't let's start this holiday in a mood.'

Lily smiled at her friends, 'Sorry, I'm a bit grumpy, still haven't got over the shock of having rotten spots on my face.'

'I know how you feel but really you can hardly see them now,' said Melanie hugging her friend.

'The train should be here in ten minutes, we have left our bikes where the porter said the guard van will stop on the platform,' said Toby.

As the train approached Lily said,

'My father said we only have to change trains in London and we should reach Rye at 3 p.m.'

When the train stopped Melanie rushed to get her bike on board, then dashed off to find the least full carriage leaving Toby to help the girls bundle their bikes into the guard van.

Melanie didn't have to go too far before she found a carriage with only one occupant. She called out to her friends,

'Come on you slow coaches, the train will soon be going.'

'Do you have to shout?' said the middle-aged city gentleman sitting in the far corner of the carriage.

Lily helped Poppy and Sarah into the carriage, following herself she fell over Poppy's rucksack which was still on the floor.

'Poppy, couldn't you have put that up on the rack?' she said in an angry voice.

Toby jumped onto the train just before the doors closed.

'That was close,' he said in a loud voice.

The man scowled at them all. Toby looked at the man's angry face and said, 'Sorry'.

'When will Ollie arrive?' asked Sarah in a whisper.

'The family only got back last night after a weeks holiday in France. They are going to drop Ollie off in Winchelsea then travel on down to Cornwall for a further two weeks holiday,' replied Toby.

They settled down to read their magazines as they had seen the passing Suffolk scenery many times before. After boarding the London train however, they watched in interest as the drab greyness of the London suburbs gradually improved as they sped deeper into the Kent countryside.

'What are those funny buildings with the peculiar shaped roofs?' asked Poppy.

'They're oasthouses, you will see lots of them as we travel through Kent. This is hop growing country and those buildings hold the kilns that dry the hops,' Toby told her.

The train pulled into Rye station on time. Lily looking out of the window shouted,

'There she is, hi, Aunt Mary, it's me, Lily.'

Her aunt ran along the platform laughing at her niece. The children climbed down from the train, said a shy hello but were put at ease when told they were all to call her Aunt Mary. She gave them all a hug, much to Toby's dismay. They hurried to get their bikes from the guard's van before he blew his whistle to depart.

Strangely enough the miserable city gent had travelled on the same trains all the way to Rye with them. Poppy saw him being picked up by a driver in a battered old van and said,

'I wouldn't have thought that's the type of man he would associate with,' as she pointed to the two men.

'Never mind them, here take your bike before the train starts to pull out,' said Toby as he passed her bike down from the van and quickly took his own, joining the girls on the platform just as the guard blew his whistle.

'How do we get back to the guest house?' Poppy asked her aunt. 'You didn't get a lorry to collect us and our bikes did you?'

Her aunt laughed,

'Goodness no, I cycled over to meet you as I only have a small car. The road out to Winchelsea Beach is flat and straight, if you had got off the train at the stop before we would have had to cycle down a very steep winding hill from old Winchelsea town. That's why you father suggested I meet you at Rye station.'

The five children wheeled their bikes out of the station and followed Aunt Mary through the town and over the bridge on the quay side. Sarah found the holiday traffic rather daunting after the quiet Suffolk lanes. She sighed in relief when they turned and cycled on the path beside the road to Winchelsea Beach.

Aunt Mary shouted back to them as she took the lead along the road through the marshes.

'These marshes once formed part of old Rye harbour, the old town of Winchelsea use to be situated near the present day Camber but was destroyed by the sea around 1288. That's why it was rebuilt on the hill.'

Cycling in single file they continued until they reached the Ship Inn, they turned into Windmill Lane and then onto a rough track which took them past the tallest thistle plants they had ever seen.

'This must be a great place for bird watching,' said Melanie as she stopped for a minute to watch the sparrows feeding off the thistles.

'Don't stop now Melanie, we have plenty of time to come out bird watching later,' said Lily.

'Here we are,' said Aunt Mary turning her bike onto the drive of the guest house.

They followed her as she led the way to a shed in the back garden.

'Park your bikes in there and I'll show you your lodgings.'

She took them through an overgrown rose arch into what Poppy immediately named to herself, *The Secret Garden*.

'Oh it's *brilliant*,' Sarah said when she saw the railway carriages.

Aunt Mary was obviously in the process of repainting them white as you could still see the old bottle green paint which she hadn't covered yet.

A full length veranda with slide back glass doors ran along the front. At right angles at either end carriages went off for the sleeping quarters.

'I'm dying to see where we sleep,' said Poppy.

'I'll show you after we have had tea. I'm sure you are

all famished after that ride from Rye.'

Her aunt slid back the veranda sliding doors to reveal a table already laid for tea.

Plates piled high with bread and butter, ham and a lovely sticky gingerbread were covered in cling-film awaiting their return.

'Sit down and help yourselves, I'll just get the bowl of salad from the fridge.'

They didn't need to be told twice but were soon tucking into the lovely meal with enthusiasm.

'There is plenty of food in the cupboard and fridge. I'm afraid you will have to fend for yourselves in the morning as I have eight guests to cook breakfast for but I'll be able to help with your lunches and make the evening meal,' she told them.

Toby, Sarah and Poppy cleared the table whilst Melanie and Lily washed and dried the dishes in the tiny kitchen.

'Now come on I know Sarah and Poppy are dying to see where they are going to sleep.'

They followed her from the veranda into the tiny kitchen and through to an equally thin but longer lounge. From this she opened the door into a corridor and showed them the bathroom, a small bunk room and a slightly longer room for Lily and Melanie to share.

'Oh, I hope you want to sleep on the top bunk, I'm not very good at heights,' said Sarah.

'I was hoping I could have the top one,' replied Poppy happily.

Aunt Mary told Toby that the boy's carriage was a mirror image of the girls but reached from the other end of the veranda.

She took a pile of maps off a shelf and put them on the table saying.

'These maps should help you explore the area by bike. They show all the public footpaths but I should warn you that the tracks across the marshes are only accessible on foot.'

They started to open the maps and have a look but Aunt Mary went on to say,

'You can have a good look at the maps in the morning before your friend Ollie arrives. Why don't you all have a good walk along the seashore, it will put some clean air into your lungs after sitting in a dirty train for hours.'

They all agreed to the walk and as they left the veranda Toby turned to her and said,

'Thank you for having us all here, I'm sure we are making you a lot of extra work.'

'Don't be daft, it's not often I have a chance to see my nieces and I'm sure I'm going to enjoy their friends' company too. Now off you go for that walk,' she said as she hurried them out of the door.

They followed the track from the guest house towards the sea, this bought them onto a tarmac road which ran parallel to the shore. They climbed concrete steps up to the sea wall which held back the shingle beach.

'What a terrific place to live but I bet it's a bit bleak in the winter,' said Melanie.

The beach stretched for miles and down the coast could be seen the silhouette of the Dungeness power station.

Toby said,

'I noticed from those maps that there are lots of tracks across the marshes to old Winchelsea town. I bet a lot of smuggling went on years ago from this beach to the old town.'

'I bet it still does, remember that fisherman last year?' said Poppy.

'Oh, yes, I don't fancy meeting anyone like him again, he was scary,' said Sarah.

'Poppy's right,' put in Melanie. 'We are always reading in our own local papers about smuggling in and out of Felixstowe docks so I expect it could easily go on here.'

'Goodness, look how far we have come, that is actually the footpath across to old Winchelsea, we had better turn back or Aunt Mary will have a search party out for us,' said Lily.

They retraced their steps along the sea wall. All the talk about smugglers and paths across the marshes had fired up Toby's imagination.

'We will have to take a packed lunch and go and explore those tracks when Ollie's here,' he suggested.

The girls readily agreed with him.

Aunt Mary was on the veranda, the table set for dinner. She sighed with relief when she saw them.

'I was beginning to think you had got lost. The dinner's ready to dish up, then I think a quick shower and an early night.'

No one disagreed; they all felt tired after the busy day and the long walk in the sea air.

When Aunt Mary had gone back to the main house they sat and looked at the maps for a time, but when they noticed Sarah rubbing her eyes everyone decided it was time for bed.

Who knows, perhaps to dream of smugglers!

3

Ollie arrives

Melanie woke early Sunday morning, she dressed quietly so as not to wake Lily who was dead to the world and gently snoring. Closing the door softly she went out into the kitchen, made a cup of tea and took it into the veranda to drink. It was so peaceful sitting at the table watching the birds feeding off the tall thistles which grew in this neglected part of the garden.

She hadn't been sitting there long when a sleepy Lily walked in rubbing her eyes.

'What on earth time is it?' she asked yawning.

'7 a.m..'

'Goodness, I never get up until eight normally in the holidays,' Lily declared.

Behind her followed a fully dressed Sarah, who said,

'Is it breakfast time? I'm famished. This sea air must be giving me an appetite.'

'I'd better lay the table then,' said Melanie getting up. 'Mind you I don't know how much food is left in the fridge after yesterday.'

'I'll go and give Poppy a shake and get dressed myself,' said Lily as she squeezed past Melanie in the kitchen.

Sarah helped lay the table then opened the door into

the other carriage and shouted,

'Come on Toby, It's 7.30 and breakfast is ready.'

Toby put in an appearance just before Lily returned with Poppy. It looked as if he had dressed in a hurry; his hair was smooth at the front but with lots of tufts stuck up at the back where he had been laying on it.

'What's wrong with your hair?' asked Lily. 'It's all matted at the back.'

'No it isn't,' said Melanie, defending Toby loyally.

'That's what comes from being woken up at an unearthly hour of the morning. I must admit I did rush a bit when Sarah called me,' Toby replied.

'Oh, stop squabbling you lot, have a glass of orange juice, it's lovely and cold, that will wake you up,' said Poppy as she gulped back a large glassful.

'What time does Ollie get here?' Lily asked Toby.

'It takes about three and half hours to drive down from Suffolk, so I expect they will arrive about noon.'

'That's right,' said Aunt Mary stepping into the veranda. 'I've promised to make dinner for them all before they set off to Cornwall. I'll cook in the house as there's more room.'

'I'll help you Aunt Mary, otherwise it will be too much work cooking for all of us and Ollie's family,' said Lily.

'That's very kind of you Lily, but don't forget I'm use to cooking for my guests. Now I suggest that you clear away the breakfast things, then put on your swimming costumes and go down to the beach for the morning. As soon as Ollie arrives I'll send him and his brother and sisters down the beach to find you.'

Aunt Mary laughed as they all tried to thank her at once, but they didn't need a second telling and twenty minutes later they were busy spreading their towels on the beach. It was a beautiful morning with large white clouds billowing across a perfect blue sky. The pebbles were hard on their feet as they went down to the sea. Toby waded out then dived in the cold water and started swimming. Melanie and Lily went in up to their waists and stood watching Toby's powerful strokes as he followed the shoreline for safety.

Sarah and Poppy were happy making sandcastles and collecting shells to decorate the walls. They swam and sunbathed alternatively and towards the end of the morning Lily came out of the sea holding a tiny crab by its leg.

'Look girls, see what I've found,' she called as she approached them.

Sarah screamed and ran away.

'Lily you know Sarah hates creepy, crawlies,' her sister said with a scowl on her face.

'I thought she would be ok with it, after all she did join us when we entered the crabbing competition last year.'

Toby had heard Sarah's scream and was coming up the beach towards them when they all heard a shout.

'Oh, it's Ollie,' shouted Poppy as a dark head appeared over the sea wall.

A tanned Ollie came into full view followed by his brother Johnny and their small twin sisters.

'Hi, everyone,' said Ollie as he strode down the beach to meet them.

Sarah and Poppy rushed up to him and gave him a hug, he looked up at Lily as the girls clung to his arms and with a slightly embarrassed look on his face said,

'It was very good of you to get your parents to include me in your holiday here.'

Lily blushed, muttered some reply whilst Poppy nudged Sarah in the ribs and gave her a wink.

The older four sat on the seawall and listened to Ollie's account of his French holiday whilst Johnny helped the four younger girls extend the size of the sandcastle.

On their return to the guest house they had to cross a "field of pebbles". It looked so odd as it was set well back from the sea front. Johnny wondered how the pebbles had got there. Toby explained that many years ago, before the sea wall had been built they were swept there by a very strong tide.

The three adults were sitting talking at a long table when the children walked in. Aunt Mary had pushed her dining tables together so that there would be room for everyone.

Ollie's parents greeted his friends, then suggested they quickly wash their hands as Lily's aunt was waiting to dish up the dinner.

Lunch was a noisy affair, with everyone talking at once. When it was time to leave, Aunt Mary wouldn't accept Ollie's mother's offer to help wash up.

'I've plenty of help,' she said nodding in the direction of the six children.

They all went outside.

Ollie's father was removing Ollie's bike from the rack at the back of the Landrover.

Goodbyes were said and as the car began to drive away Ollie's mother put her head out of the window and called,

'Now don't get into any mischief, whilst we are away, will you?'

Mischief, no, but adventure, well maybe, we shall see!

4

Making plans

The children spent the afternoon on the veranda, poring over the maps, trying to decide which route to take the next day for their walk.

'I vote we go over the marshes to Winchelsea town,' said Toby. 'We can take a packed lunch with us and buy ice-cream and drinks there,' he continued.

'How far is it?' Lily asked. 'Don't forget Poppy only has little legs.'

'I have not,' shouted Poppy, giving her sister a push.

'Poppy's OK, she never complains of being tired even when she is,' said Toby.

Poppy gave Toby her sweetest smile.

'I should think it's about two to three miles right into the town, and if we come back by the road we can take a short cut across the fields which will be safer and quicker,' said Toby.

'Sarah and me will be the scouts, thrashing a path through the marshes,' said Poppy swinging her rounders bat back and forward, nearly hitting Ollie in the shins.

'You will both keep behind me; I don't want you two falling into any dykes,' replied Toby.

'Have you still got your binoculars?' Ollie asked Melanie.

'Of course I have, you never know we may come across some rare birds on the marshes. I'll bring them with me.'

Aunt Mary popped in to see them and said,

'It's a bit late in the day to go too far now but why don't you take a walk and have a look at Camber Castle. It's easy to find, you just follow the track outside the house which brings you to a stile and you are practically there.'

They all agreed it was a good idea and followed her out of the door.

'Can we have a packed lunch tomorrow as we want to be out all day?' Lily asked her aunt.

'Of course you can, I'll bring over extra supplies after breakfast and help you. I've got a busy day tomorrow so I won't have to worry about you if we pack up plenty of food.'

They waved goodbye and set off down the track. Along one side were odd bungalows of all shapes and sizes. Some were just wooden shacks, some had been modernised and improved. Most looked like holiday homes, quiet and empty of people.

They faced the sea across the marshes, the seashore hidden from the track by the high sea wall.

'Look at that bungalow,' said Poppy. 'Its walls are covered in sea shells; there must be thousands of them.'

'I like that row of swans along the bottom of the front wall,' said Sarah pointing.

The boys went nearer to inspect the end wall which depicted a large white horse upon which sat a knight in armour. They all agreed that the walls must have taken ages to complete.

They continued along the track, which became narrower with hardly room for one car to navigate its ruts and potholes. The trees either side of the track met overhead and the children felt as if they were entering a dark green tunnel.

'It's very quiet,' whispered Poppy, reaching for Sarah's hand.

They came to another track, which crossed the one they were on. Two men were talking by a scruffy white van. The taller of the two had red hair and they heard him say to his companion,

'I've got one more job to do tomorrow.'

Becoming aware of the children whose approach had been softened by the grass growing on the track, he looked at Toby and Ollie and said,

'What are you kids doing here? This is private land, *CLEAR OFF.*'

'It's a public right of way, we have as much right to be here as you do,' replied Toby.

'*CLEAR OFF* I say or I'll give you a cuff around the ear!'

The man snarled at them, gripped his companion's arm and walked around to the side of the van, whispering earnestly.

'What a horrid man,' said Melanie as they hurried away down the lane.

'Did you notice the red-haired man's eyebrows? They were jet black, not red, and *very* bushy,' said Sarah.

'Yes, but didn't any of you notice his companion? It was the rough looking man that picked up the city gent at Rye,' said Poppy.

'You're right, so it was, agreed Lily who then gave Ollie details of their fellow travelling companion from Suffolk.

The men were most unpleasant characters and they hoped they wouldn't run into them again but they were soon forgotten as they climbed the style and Camber Castle came into view.

'*Wow,*' said Ollie.

'*Great!*' said Toby.

Both imagined themselves defending the town of Rye from the castle battlements in the years long gone by.

'It's really marvellous; I can just imagine a knight in shining armour coming to rescue me from the battlements,' said Lily with a sigh.

Toby and Ollie looked at each other, laughed and Toby said,

'It's much more likely that they stood at those slit windows, firing arrows at enemies from the sea.'

'You must admit it looks very romantic though,' put in Melanie.

The castle did look imposing but rather strange, as it was set in the middle of a large field full of sheep.

'This spit of land was known as Cobble Point,' Toby informed them.

Ollie looked impressed until Lily pointed out rather rudely that Toby had been swatting up on the area before he left home.

They had a good look around the ruins and then headed back the same way. There was no sign of the two men when they reached the junction of the tracks, much to everyone's relief.

'I'm glad those horrid men have gone,' said Poppy.

'So am I,' replied Sarah. 'It wasn't as if we were doing any harm, was it?'

It was nearly dusk by the time the children got back. Aunt Mary was on the veranda laying the table for tea.

'Oh, there you are, come on in and wash your hands. It won't take me long to make sandwiches.'

Aunt Mary was surprised at how quiet they all were at teatime. The sea air, swimming and the long afternoon walk must have tired them all out she thought.

That evening they played cards and board games until Aunt Mary popped in at 9 p.m. and suggested they have an early night. Nobody complained, after all it had been a very tiring day.

And nobody knew just what tomorrow would bring!

5

Monday morning

Monday morning proved to be just as nice as Sunday.

They arose early, keen to get on their way. When Aunt Mary arrived they had already washed up and made their beds.

'I've left my kitchen as it was, it can all wait until later,' she said preparing to cut piles of sandwiches.

Melanie and Lily were given the task of wrapping up cake in cling-film and sorting out apples and bananas whilst they boys packed everything into small backpacks.

'Do you want to take drinks with you?' Aunt Mary asked.

'No thanks,' said Lily, we'll get them in the town when we get there, we won't have so much to carry then.'

Bags packed together with wet weather gear. Toby had the Ordnance Survey map in a plastic wallet hanging around his neck. They were ready to set off.

'Expect us when you see us,' called Poppy as she waved to her aunt.

'We *will* be back in time for tea,' Sarah said, stressing the word will.

They decided to walk along the sea wall rather than on the lower tarmac road.

Even though it was a lovely August morning, the beach was almost deserted. The occasional person could be seen walking their dog and one or two joggers overtook them as they passed Smeatons Harbour. Actually there wasn't a harbour there at all anymore, just a pile of old timber beams and rubble lying on the beach.

'Come on,' said Toby. 'We carry on pass these holiday caravan parks and the footpath should soon start going over the marshes.'

Sarah and Poppy had gone on ahead. They stopped and Poppy shouted back,

'Here it is, we cross the style here and the sign post points in the direction of that white house over there in the distance, just below old Winchelsea.'

Toby and Ollie checked the map and agreed it was the correct path. Climbing over styles and dodging the sheep which scattered madly at their approach, they made their way over the marsh keeping the white house in sight.

They crossed the bridge over the disused Royal Military Canal.

'This would make a good spot for fishing,' Toby said turning to Ollie.

'We are not spending our precious holiday watching you two fish, I don't mind crabbing, that's fun, but sitting there all day waiting for a fish to bite is too boring for words,' said Lily.

'Let's stop for a breather and watch the swans,' said Melanie noticing how quiet Sarah had become.

Sarah gave Melanie a grateful smile and flopped down on the grass; Poppy, needing no second bidding followed.

Realising why Melanie had suggested a stop, the others stopped, Ollie unpacked one of the sandwiches and fed the swans.

'Hey that's our lunch,' said Poppy.

'Yes we will need all our strength to cross this marsh,' put in Sarah.

The older four laughed at the outraged look on the two young girls' faces as the swans gobbled up the sandwiches.

'It's clouding over, we had better get on our way. If it rains we haven't anywhere to shelter out here on the marshes,' said Toby.

As they neared the end of the footpath the sky darkened and large raindrops began to fall.

'Quick let's get over the last style onto the road,' said Ollie. 'There's a large oak tree there. I think we should be ok to shelter under it.'

The sky got darker as the rain became steadily heavier. They managed to reach the tree before they got completely soaked. This tree stood on a grass verge about five yards from a very high red brick wall. They had been sheltering under the large, spreading branches for not more than ten minutes when they heard a scratching sound coming from the other side of the wall.

To the children's astonishment a canvas holdall came sailing over the wall and the children watched in amazement as a man hauled himself over the top, jumped down and not seeing the children, picked up the bag and dashed off down the road, disappearing out of sight around the bend.

'Did you see who that was?' Lily asked excitedly.

'Bushy eyebrows,' Poppy and Sarah said together.

'Even in this light you couldn't mistake his bright red hair,' added Ollie.

'What's he been up to?' Melanie said.

'No good you can be sure, I know let's follow him,' said Toby.

He dashed off down the road followed closely behind by the others. The rain had stopped but they didn't notice that as they turned the bend in the road towards Winchelsea to find the road empty, Not a sign of the man anywhere.

'Look, these tyre marks here on the verge, I bet he went off by car,' said Ollie.

'Or van,' muttered Poppy.

'Well, we have lost him now so we might as well carry on into Winchelsea. I could do with a cold drink,' said Toby.

They carried on walking down the narrow road into the old town and entered through one of the old remaining gates called New Gate.

They found a shop in which they were able to buy tins of drink.

'We can go and eat our lunch at the look out by the Strand Gate; they say it has a marvellous view across the marshes to the sea beyond Winchelsea Beach. You can also see Camber Castle,' said Toby.

'Another snippet of information from your guide book Toby,' said Lily.

Toby ignored this remark and led the way. He was right, the view was terrific and just the place to stop for lunch.

'Do you think we should go and tell the police about

Bushy eyebrows?' asked Ollie sensibly.

'I was just thinking that myself,' Toby replied.

'We can find out where the police station is from that street map on the board outside the church,' put in Melanie.

They packed up the remains of their lunch and empty drink cans and retraced their steps to the church.

'Here it is,' said Melanie pointing to the board. 'Look, it's just two streets from here.'

The old town of Winchelsea was planned on a series of 'blocks' similar to the American system, this made it rather confusing when walking around the town trying to find a certain street without a street map.

The police station looked like an ordinary cottage from the outside, only the sign above the door told you otherwise.

'I'll do the talking,' said Toby as they filed through the door.

The police sergeant looked up to find six children of various sizes peering at him with anxious looks on their faces.

'I think I had better start by saying, *Hello, hello, hello, what's all this*?' he said smiling at them. 'Are you lost?'

Toby, pleased to find a friendly adult said, 'We want to report an unusual incident sir.'

'Right then,' said the sergeant, drawing a large red book towards himself. 'Let's start with your names and addresses first shall we?'

Toby gave him this information and then told him all about the red-haired man, adding how they had also seen him and another man the previous day on the way to Camber Castle. He also mentioned the man on the train.

The sergeant wrote everything down. He finished writing, looked up at them and said,

'Well done, you were right to report this, I'll look into things at Rother Hall.'

Seeing their questioning glances, he explained,

'That is the name of the house where you say the man jumped over the wall. If anything comes to light, I dare say we will need to question you all again. Now off you go and enjoy the rest of your holiday,' he smiled waving them out of the station.

'Well that's that then,' said Ollie.

'What do we do now?' Lily asked.

'Go back for tea,' replied Poppy and Sarah together.

'You greedy guts, you have only just had lunch,' exclaimed Melanie.

'When I said *what do we do now*,' replied Lily, 'I meant about old Bushy eyebrows.'

'We will all have to keep our eyes open for him and if we do see him we will have to follow him to find out where he lives,' said Toby.

'Gosh I fancy a bit of sleuthing,' said Ollie. 'I hope I spot him first.'

'We will have to take care; we already know what a nasty character he is. We don't know what he might do if he finds us spying on him,' Toby said seriously.

'Yes, remember what happened to you five last year at Southwold,' said Ollie.*

'I said we would have another adventure,' exclaimed Poppy.

They went back to the Strand Gate and down the hill

towards Rye. This was the main Hastings road so they had to be careful, the pavement was narrow and the traffic very busy.

'I'll go first, then Poppy and Sarah, Melanie and Lily with Ollie bringing up the rear,' said Toby.

'Aye, aye, Captain,' saluted Ollie with a grin.

When they reached the Bridge Inn at the bottom of the hill the path became a bit wider. They turned right over the Royal Military Canal towards Winchelsea Beach.

Looking at the map again, Toby said,

'We can take a footpath across the fields and cut out following the road for a good way.'

Sarah could feel the hot sun beating down upon her head. She sighed in relief when they re-joined the road. A nearby shop was advertising, *locally caught fish.*

Poppy turned and called to Ollie,

'If we went fishing tomorrow we could have our own fish for tea.'

Sarah groaned, now she really felt sick.

'Huh,' snorted Lily. 'You won't fill your stomach on the tiddlers you would catch.'

'We don't want to go fishing, we want to go out with Melanie's binoculars and look for Bushy eyebrows,' said Toby.

As much as Ollie would have loved to have gone fishing, he reluctantly agreed with what Toby had said.

Thank goodness thought Sarah as they finally turned into Windmill Lane then down the track to the guest house.

Aunt Mary couldn't understand what they were trying to tell her as they rushed up to her in the garden.

'Slow down, one at a time,' she said.

Lily told her aunt of their meeting with the two men the day before and of seeing Bushy eyebrows again near old Winchelsea town. Although surprised by their story Aunt Mary was rather worrid.

'Now don't you go looking for these men, they could be dangerous. Come and tell me if you see them and I'll telephone the police. Don't forget I'm responsible for you all while you are away from home. Goodness I thought this was a peaceful part of the country.'

Exhausted they lay down on the grass while Aunt Mary went to prepare the evening meal.

see The Southwold Adventure.

6

Headline news

The next morning Lily and Melanie awoke about the same time, they dressed quietly as there was no sound from Poppy and Sarah's room.

Toby and Ollie were drinking tea on the veranda.

'You two are up early, aren't you?' said Lily.

'We are waiting for the local paper to be delivered,' said Toby.

'What for?' asked Melanie, who hadn't quite woken up and wasn't thinking clearly.

'To see if there is any report of a break in at Rother Hall, of course,' Toby replied.

'I bet there is,' Lily said.

'Aren't Poppy and Sarah up yet? Poppy keeps on about fishing so I was going to suggest that we go at night. That way you and Melanie won't miss a single days holiday,' said Ollie.

'I wouldn't mind going night fishing,' replied Melanie.

'Well you can count me out,' said Lily crossly as she stormed off to wake up Poppy and Sarah. She hated being left out of things but she was determined not to give in and go with them.

Just then the van delivering the papers arrived and Toby rushed to meet it. He practically grabbed the newspaper from the man's hand. The man raised his eyebrows, turned away muttering, something which sounded like, 'youngsters of today have no manners'.

Toby, shamefaced, came back into the garden. Melanie and Ollie tried to look over his shoulder as he unfolded the newspaper.

'*Wow...*' was all Toby muttered, his eyes wide in astonishment. '*Look...*' he lowered the newspaper so they could see the headlines, which read:-

ROBBERY AT ROTHER HALL

He read out:-

'The home of Colonel and Mrs. Derwent was burgled yesterday whilst they were on holiday in Scotland.

According to their housekeeper the safe had been opened and valuable jewellery had been taken.'

The report went on,

'The police state that they have witnesses as to the time of the theft and also a very good description of a man seen leaving the premises in a suspicious manner.'

Just then Aunt Mary came out of her kitchen to ask what all the noise was about. Toby gave her the newspaper so that she could read the article herself.

'Well I never, let's hope the police soon catch them, I must go and get on with the guest's breakfast but I'll be over for a chat as soon as they go out.' And with that she dashed back to the house.

The three walked back down the garden towards the railway carriages.

'That must be us the police are referring to as witnesses,' said Ollie.

Lily was at the veranda doorway.

'What's all the noise about?' Lily asked.

She had already forgotten about being annoyed over the night fishing.

Sarah and Poppy pushed past her and Poppy rushed up to Toby and tried to tug the newspaper out of his hand.

'Is there any mention of a robbery?'

Toby quickly read out the article for their benefit.

Breakfast was a noisy affair, the newspaper article was read several times over.

As the day promised to be another hot one, they decided to go swimming early before the sun was overhead.

They were just about to set off when a police car drew up and out climbed the sergeant from Winchelsea plus two other men in plain clothes.

'I'm Detective Chief Inspector Bennett from Reginal HQ and this is Sergeant Cross,' he said indicating the other man in plain clothes.

'Sergeant Waters, I believe you met at Winchelsea police station yesterday.'

Aunt Mary came round from the front door when she heard strange men's voices.

'Oh, it's the police,' she said.

'Yes Madam,' DCI Bennett said, approaching Aunt Mary and extending his hand.

'I take it that you need to question the children again, come into the dining room there's more room there.'

She showed them into the room and said,

'Shall I make a pot of tea?'

'Yes please, this can be thirsty work,' said the DCI with a smile.

'I'll start to take the children's statements again. You never know they may be able to recall something they hadn't mentioned before.'

The grown-ups drank tea whilst the children gave their statements and when they had all been questioned Toby asked,

'Have you any idea as to who the red-haired man might be?'

'Your description does fit a well-known thief who was released from prison nine months ago. He came from the London area but nothing has been seen or heard of him since then.'

This information came from Sergeant Cross, who until now had only written down their statements.

'There have been a lot of burglaries in the area over the past six months and we now think the red-haired man to be responsible,' said the DCI.

'I can't tell you his name of course but it should only be a matter of time before we catch him. We think his accomplice may be a local man and we have put out a description of him.'

He got up, followed by the two sergeants.

'Don't forget to let me know immediately if you catch sight of either of them,' he said as they walked down the path to their car.

Aunt Mary said she had to get on and finish painting the railway carriages so the children picked up their towels yet again and spent the morning swimming and sunbathing.

7

A busy afternoon

When they returned for lunch they found Aunt Mary fast asleep lying on a sun lounger under an elderberry tree in the back garden. She still had white paint on her cheek and glasses.

'Oh dear, I expect we have tired her out with all the extra meals she has had to make. I think we should help her this afternoon,' said Poppy.

'Good idea, I feel ashamed that I didn't think of it first,' her sister replied.

The others agreed and Lily said,

'Let's start by getting lunch ready ourselves, I know what Aunt Mary was going to give us today.'

They all crept back to the front veranda and Lily set each of them a task. Sarah and Poppy laid the table and set out the cutlery. Melanie prepared a large bowl of salad, placing it in the centre of the table. Toby and Ollie made a pile of sandwiches much to the girls surprise. When everything was ready Lily put a large pot of tea, made just the way her aunt liked it onto the table.

Sarah and Poppy went to wake Aunt Mary.

'Come on, lunch is ready,' Poppy said gently shaking her aunt.

Aunt Mary sat up, rubbed her eyes then cleaned the paint from her glasses.

'Right then, lead me to it,' she said with a smile on her face.

When she saw the table all ready laid for lunch, she looked at them all and wiped a tear from her eye.

'We are going to help you this afternoon, what can we do for you?' Poppy asked.

'Well dear I've finally finished the paintwork on the rest of the carriages but I would like a few small flower borders to the side of the veranda and front carriage.

Some colourful plants will show nicely against the new white paint. If you would all like to do that after lunch, I'll go into Rye and buy the plants, then this afternoon when the sun goes down a bit we can plant them,' she said.

Everyone enjoyed the lunch especially as they had prepared it themselves. They cleared away and washed the dishes and as Aunt Mary set off in her car they went looking in the shed for gardening tools.

It was quite hard work digging as there were lots of pebbles in the garden. Poppy and Sarah were given the task of collecting them whilst the others did the digging.

They worked solidly for several hours and by the time Aunt Mary came back there were several neat borders along the front of the veranda and carriage.

When the car pulled into the drive the children came over to help unload the plants.

'You have done well,' she told them.

'You all look very hot and bothered, go and sit down, I'll bring out some cold lemonade and a plate of those nice biscuits I made yesterday.

They flopped down on the grass and lay there for an hour whilst they waited for the sun to go down.

Aunt Mary bought out the refreshments, gave instructions as to which plants were to go where and then left them to go and prepare the evening meal.

8

Fishing

That evening they were playing cards when Aunt Mary popped in to see them.

'Would it be ok for us to go fishing tonight?' Ollie asked her.

'Yes, but not Sarah and Poppy, they are a bit too young to be out late at night.'

'That's ok,' Poppy said, 'Sarah doesn't really like fishing and I don't think either of us will be able to keep our eyes open that late anyway.'

'Do you boys mind if I tag along? I haven't got a fishing rod but I'd like to sit out on the beach at night,' Melanie asked them.

'Of course you can come, I know you can keep quiet,' Toby said looking in Lily's direction.

Lily scowled back at him. She was feeling a bit peeved, she really would have liked to have gone fishing with them but after her comments about fishing that morning she felt she couldn't do anything but stay behind.

About ten thirty, long after Poppy and Sarah had gone to bed, the boys and Melanie started to sort out the fishing tackle, torches and to make up some flasks of coffee.

'Put warm jumpers on,' Aunt Mary told them. 'It will be quite chilly on the beach tonight. Take the key with you Toby as Lily and me will go to bed when you've gone. Please make sure you lock up when you get back.'

Toby, Ollie and Melanie finally left at eleven p.m. watched by Lily.

An owl hooted as they crunched along the track, crossed the tarmac road and climbed the steps up to the sea wall.

The full moon was occasionally blocked out by a passing cloud.

The boys selected a place to put up their fishing tackle and Melanie sat down happy just to listen to the waves and watch the clouds passing across the moon.

The boys didn't seem to be having much luck and by midnight they had only caught a few small fish.

'Oh, I've had enough,' said Ollie. 'Let's call it a night and go back.'

'OK, I've not had as much luck as you,' Toby said, throwing back yet another small fish into the sea.

They packed up their tackle, Melanie collected the flask and rug and they trudged back over the beach. They had just turned into the guest house garden when they heard a cough. The children stopped and quickly ducked down behind the fence when they saw the man's face illuminated as he struck a match to light a cigarette. He then moved on up the track towards the tarmac road.

'Did you recognise him?' Whispered Ollie.

'Yes, it's the man's red-haired companion isn't it?' Toby replied.

'Shush, I think he is coming back again,' Melanie said

as they heard the sound of feet on the gravel.

The man passed them again, muttering to himself, 'where's he got to?'

'Come on,' said Ollie, 'We've got to follow him, he might lead us to Bushy eyebrows.'

They left the fishing tackle on the grass and keeping to the grassy strip in the middle of the track, they followed the man at a safe distance.

It was quite easy as they could smell his cigarette and hear his smoker's cough.

Instead of following the track into Windmill Lane he turned left. When the children turned the corner he had disappeared into what seemed to be a dead end.

'He must have gone into one of these bungalows, but which one?' said Toby.

'No I don't think so,' said Melanie. 'See that gate there, it's a public right of way through the Homesteads, I think he has taken that. Come on.'

The gate opened onto a path that was only three feet wide. To one side was a chestnut fence with spindly saplings planted on the adjoining plot of land and to the other side was an enormously tall conifer hedge. The owner of that property had recently trimmed the hedge. They walked in single file down the dark alleyway, the conifer clippings deadening the sound of their footsteps.

They came to another gate which led onto an unmade road but here the road went to the right and left. The clouds had covered the moon again and it was pitch black.

Ollie sniffed the air.

'I think it's to the right,' he said.

'Look he must have stopped to re-light his cigarette, I can see a faint glow,' said Melanie.

Walking forward cautiously, they stopped when they heard a gate creak. Then a sharp rap on a door, some whispered muttering, the sound of a door being opened and closed.

They drew level with a white gate whose paint was badly peeling and the hinges practically hanging off.

'Yes this is the gate,' said Toby. 'There's a smouldering cigarette on the ground.' He stubbed it out with the toe of his shoe.

'What do we do now?' asked Melanie.

'Stay here, I'll try to get near to the window,' said Toby. 'There's a gap in those tatty old curtains, and the glass in the fanlight window has a large piece missing, I might be able to hear what they say.'

Melanie and Ollie stood in complete silence as Toby, keeping to the lawn followed the path to the front window. He climbed upon some bricks which supported a water-butt. He was pleased to find that the torn curtains gave him a good view into the room. 'Bushy eyebrows' was standing sideways to Toby. He was looking across the room and saying to the other man,

'I couldn't risk coming out tonight to meet you, didn't you read today's papers? The police say they have a description of me and witnesses.'

'What about yesterday's haul, where's that?' the other man asked. 'I've brought the money from the "fence" in London for the last lot I gave him. He is eager to see the next lot of jewels,' continued the man handing over a packet to "Bushy eyebrows".

'Don't you worry, I've got them safely hidden away

but not here. I have got to get away from this area. It's too hot for me now. My pal is picking me up tomorrow night and driving me to Dover. I can mingle with the holiday-makers going to France and lay low for a long time on what I've made in the past six months.'

'What about my share of the money,' said the other man.

'Tell the "fence" to give you your cut and to keep the rest for me until I send for it,' replied Bushy eyebrows.

'Where shall I meet you and what time?' the accomplice asked.

Bushy eyebrows laughed and said,

'Believe it or not, I'm going to cross the marshes and my pal will be waiting for me in a lay-by just outside the wall of the last house I robbed. I'll meet you there to hand over the jewels. I can't risk getting them too soon. You take the van and meet me at the lay-by at midnight. You will see my pal's Landrover waiting there.'

'What was that?' hissed the accomplice.

Toby had felt something soft brush against his leg. He jumped down off the bricks and dislodged the gravel under his feet.

Melanie and Ollie looked at each other in fright as the front door shot open and light spilled out onto the path. They ducked down behind the hedge.

The robber's red hair glowed in the light of the hall lamp. He bent down and laughed as he picked up a black cat and turned back to the other man saying,

'Trouble with us Dick, we are getting too jumpy, it's only the stray cat I've been feeding.'

Toby slowly got up from crouching behind the water-butt. Beads of perspiration ran down his forehead as he retraced his steps along the side of the path to rejoin Melanie and Ollie.

'Let's get away from here quickly and I'll tell you all I've heard,' he whispered.

When they had safely retraced their steps through the alleyway, Toby recounted the robber's plans to them as they listened in amazement.

'You know what we have to do?' Melanie said. 'We must wake up Aunt Mary and get her to telephone the police as soon as possible.'

They both agreed with her as they hurried back. They were in such a rush that they fell over the fishing tackle on the path as they entered the garden of the guest house. The noise they made aroused Aunt Mary.

'Goodness, what time is this to be coming back? It's nearly two a.m.!' Aunt Mary exclaimed.

'I'm very sorry but come down to the veranda as the girls will want to hear what we have to tell you,' said Toby.

The light was already on in the veranda and Lily was looking out of the door.

'I wondered what all the noise was but why is Aunt Mary up at this time of night?' Lily wanted to know.

Just then a sleepy Poppy and Sarah appeared.

'What's all the noise?' Poppy asked.

'Sit down everyone whilst Toby tells you what we discovered tonight,' said Melanie.

Lily was livid as the story unfolded.

'You rotters, you've had an adventure without us. We've missed all the excitement,' she wailed.

Aunt Mary said,

'I think I had better telephone the police right now,

even though it's the middle of the night.'

She got up and went to the telephone. The children listened, hearing her asking for DCI Bennett.

'Yes, I said *urgent*,' she said impatiently. 'I know it's the middle of the night, please put me through to him at home then, tell him it's in connection with the recent robberies and that the children from Winchelsea Beach have some very important information to pass on to him.'

There was a long pause and then they heard her say,

'I'm sorry it's so late Detective Chief Inspector but I really thought or rather the children thought that I should telephone you without delay.'

She retold the story to DCI Bennett. There was another pause.

'Yes, I'll send them to bed now and I'll make sure they are up first thing in the morning before you get here, goodnight.'

She replaced the telephone and said, 'DCI Bennett will be here at 9 a.m. so off to bed now, there will be plenty of time for talking in the morning.'

Toby and Ollie went off to their carriage talking excitedly whilst Sarah and Poppy continued to question Melanie as they made their way to bed.

Lily pretended not to be interested but she followed on behind listening intently, a scowl still on her face.

Let's hope she is in a better mood in the morning!

9

The police arrive

Even though they had not gone to bed until nearly 3 a.m., all the children were up early, showered, dressed and had breakfast by 8.45 a.m.

Everyone was waiting on the veranda eagerly listening for a car. At last the police turned up, this time it was only DCI Bennett and Sergeant Cross.

'Good morning,' said the DCI. 'I hear you have had an exciting night.'

He sat down at the table and Sergeant Cross took out his note-book, licked his pencil and waited.

'Right Toby let's have an account of all that happened last night,' said the DCI.

Toby ran through his story again, prompted in places by Ollie and Melanie.

Lily and Poppy kept silent, they were still annoyed at missing all the excitement. Sarah was secretly glad they had missed everything.

Sergeant Cross continued silently writing everything down, only looking up every now and then, as if he found it hard to believe the children's story.

'You acted bravely, even though it was a bit foolish. Those men might have turned nasty if they had caught you,' DCI Bennett said when he had all the facts.

'I'm not familiar with all those tracks and footpaths across the marshes. Can you show me on the map?' he asked.

'I'll get the map,' said Melanie, going into the lounge.

Everyone started asking questions at once.

'Hold on there, one at a time.'

Melanie returned and gave him the map. Toby pointed out the foopath across the marshes and the spot where the Landrover and the white van were to park.

'Good we will be ready for them,' said DCI Bennett.

'Can we come?' Ollie and Toby asked together.

'Certainly not, this is police work and could turn out to be dangerous. Don't worry though, I'll be over personally to give you a full report. It if hadn't been for this information our job could have taken a lot longer. That's assuming we get them of course.'

With that he got up, shook hands with everyone and left with Sergeant Cross.

'Why don't you all go on the beach for the rest of the morning?' said Aunt Mary. 'After lunch I suggest you all have a short nap to make up for lost sleep,' she said over her shoulder as she went off to the house.

The children hurriedly collected their swimsuits and towels and ambled down to the beach. .

Everyone's mood was a bit flat after the excitement of the previous night. Towels were spread out over the pebbles and they laid down to sunbathe. Not one of them had any energy for swimming.

'I'd give anything to be there at midnight,' said Toby.

'So would I,' agreed Ollie.

'I still can't believe I missed all the excitement,' said Lily.

'Well, I just hope they catch those horrid men, we don't want to bump into them again,' said Sarah.

'It's no good us moaning and moping, let's play tag in the surf,' suggested Melanie.

'Last one in the water is a *dunce*,' shouted Ollie as he raced off over the pebbles, not seeming to feel them digging into his feet.

The children spent the next few hours having fun, the boys skimmed pebbles on the sea whilst Lily and Melanie helped build a sandcastle for Sarah and Poppy.

After a good lunch everyone was quite happy to take up Aunt Mary's suggestion of having a sleep.

Lily was awoken a few hours later by the sound of voices coming down the garden from the house. She went out into the veranda and looked in disbelief as her mother and father and Aunt Mary came into view.

'Mum, Dad,' she shrieked and flung herself into her mother's arms.

'What's all this we hear,' said her father, gently roughing her hair up.

'Oh Dad, the others went off last night without me, Poppy and Sarah and had a terrific adventure,' Lily exclaimed.

Her shriek had woken all the others, they spilled out onto the veranda.

'Mum, Dad, how come you are here?' Poppy said as she hugged her mother.

'Aunt Mary telephone us this morning whilst you were on the beach. We thought we had better come ourselves and find out what you had all been up to,' her father replied.

Aunt Mary got up and said she was going to the house

to start preparing the evening meal.

'I think I'll come and help you,' her sister-in-law said. 'You can tell me all they have been up to and 'I'll leave poor Andrew to hear the children's side of the story.'

The meal time was a very noisy affair, everyone seemed to have a healthy appetite and all plates were left empty.

They talked for ages that evening, all wondering what was going to happen outside Rother Hall at midnight.

'Right, time for bed everyone,' said Lily and Poppy's father.

'You will be having dreams of cops and robbers and chases across the marshes all night.'

Sarah knew she certainly didn't want to have bad dreams so she quickly got up to go to bed, thinking she would keep her head under the duvet that night.

'Perhaps we shall hear some good news from the police tomorrow,' said Toby as they all reluctantly said goodnight and went off to bed.

10

Caught with the goods

Thursday morning dawned bright and clear. For some reason everyone slept in except for Aunt Mary who had breakfast to cook for her guests.

She made herself a pot of tea and went to the front door. The newspaper was already sticking through the letter box.

She pulled it free and went and sat at the table in the kitchen. With a cup of tea in front of her she unfolded the paper and read the headlines.

SCHOOL CHILDREN HELP CATCH NOTORIOUS THIEF

'Goodness me!' she exclaimed as she finished reading the article. 'I had better go and wake the children.'

She ran down the garden, entered the veranda and went into the girl's carriage.

'Come on girls, get up, there's an article in the newspaper about last night's activities over at Winchelsea.'

Melanie and Lily scrambled for their clothes, whilst Poppy merely mumbled, 'What's up?'

Sarah stirred under her duvet.

'I'm off to wake the boys,' said Aunt Mary.

Toby and Ollie were already up and dressing when she popped her head around their door.

'The paper has arrived, good news too,' she said leaving the room and dropping the newspaper on the table.

'I've got to get back to my guests. I'll send the girl's parents down after breakfast,' she called out as she left.

The boys put a spurt on and dashed out of their bedroom.

'What does it say?' asked Ollie.

The girls came into the veranda and everyone crowded around Toby as he read aloud:

SCHOOL CHILDREN HELP CATCH NOTORIOUS THIEF

The police apprehended a notorious jewellery thief in the early hours of the morning after a chase across the Winchelsea marshes. The police have been trying to discover the identity of the thief for the last six months following a spate of burglaries in several large houses in the area.
It is understood, from reliable sources that they had received information from six children on holiday at Winchelsea Beach.

'*Wow*, we are famous,' said Sarah.

The others laughed but Melanie said,

'I wonder why there was a chase over the marshes?'

'Bushy eyebrows must have heard the police following him,' replied Ollie.

'I suggest we quickly have our breakfast as I expect

DCI Bennett may be over later to let us know what went on last night,' said Toby.

'I don't know about you lot but I feel very hungry,' said Poppy.

'Right then, let's get the table laid,' said Lily.

Breakfast was a quiet meal for a change; they each had their own thoughts as to what might have happened in the night.

Lily and Poppy's parents came into the veranda with Aunt Mary. Everyone wanted to be the one to read the newspaper article out loud to them.

'Toby can read it again,' said Aunt Mary in a loud voice, so as to be heard over the squabbling.

They sat on the veranda talking for most of the morning until a police car pulled up.

A beaming DCI Bennett and Sergeant Cross got out and approached the group on the veranda.

'Well children, I take it you have all read the papers this morning,' said DCI Bennett.

'Yes we have,' everyone tried to say at once.

'What happened?' asked Toby.

'As you read, we caught them, the red headed thief, his accomplice and the Landrover's driver. A good nights work due to the six of you. We even recovered the jewels from the Rother Hall burglary. Colonel and Mrs. Derwent will be pleased.'

'How did the chase over the marshes come about?' Ollie asked.

'We had men lying in wait by the lay-by near Rother Hall and a squad car hidden from view along the road. We also sent men with a police dog at a distance following the marsh footpath. Jack King, that's the thief's name must have sensed he was being followed as he suddenly started to run but luckily for us, he tripped and fell headlong into the canal.'

The children and adults all laughed. DCI Bennett continued,

'My men sent the dog in to drag him out. The commotion must have alerted the other two men waiting beside the walls of Rother Hall. They started to make a run for it. The policemen there quickly caught Jack King's accomplice but the man in the Landrover managed to drive off. He didn't stand a chance though as the squad car was informed and they gave chase. We caught up with him on the road, making for Dover.

All we need to do now is get the name of the man in London who disposed of the jewels. We think that's the man you saw on the train and with your description of him and by putting a bit of pressure on Jack King I think we should be able to get a name out of him.'

The children put several other questions to the DCI but finally all their questions answered, the two policemen rose to leave.

'I expect you will be hearing from our Chief Constable shortly as I think he will want to thank you all personally. Now I suggest you enjoy the rest of your holiday.'

He shook hands with the adults, waved to the children and got into the car and was driven off by Sergeant Cross.

The six children left the adults talking and walked down to the beach. Sitting on the sea wall Ollie turned to the others and said,

'I'm so glad you invited me, this has been a brilliant holiday so far.'

'I don't suppose we shall have another one like it,' sighed Lily.

Poppy looked at Sarah, raised her eyebrows and just smiled.

M ap of Winchelsea Beach area

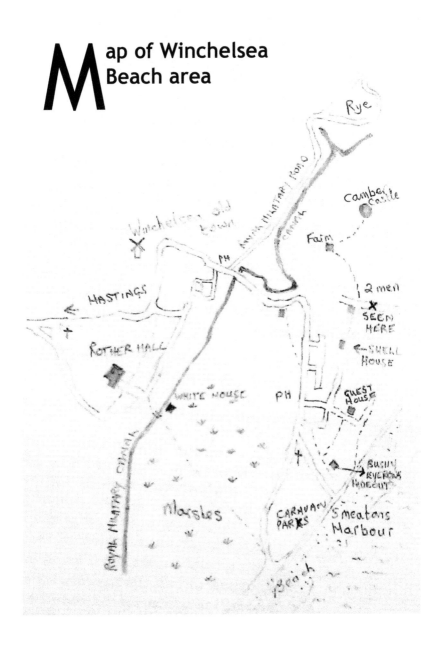

Author's note

If you ever go to Winchelsea Beach area you will be able to find many of the tracks I mention. I wrote this book some years ago but I hope that you will still be able to find the bungalow covered with shells. The track will still be there that leads you to Camber Castle and you will be able to find the New Gate and Strand Gate in old Winchelsea town.

The pebble field and the hidden footpath through the Homesteads are real, as are the names of the public houses I mention. Windmill Lane is genuine too but not the guest house. I did see some dilapidated railway carriages in an overgrown garden though.

Enjoy your holidays, and happy hunting.

Angela Taylor

Other children's books by Angela Taylor

Izzy's Quest for Gold

Finch

And for adults

A Dangerous Move

Lightning Source UK Ltd.
Milton Keynes UK
UKHW022040070919
349327UK00010B/848/P

9 781782 227052